Awesome
Athletes

Other books in the History Makers series:

History MAKERS

Awesome
Athletes

By Ron Horton

LUCENT
BOOKS®

THOMSON
GALE

San Diego • Detroit • New York • San Francisco • Cleveland
New Haven, Conn. • Waterville, Maine • London • Munich

Cover: Champion surfer Kelly Slater gets barreled in Fiji.

LIBRARY OF CONGRESS CATALOGING-IN-PUBLICATION DATA

Horton, Ron (Ronald Everett)
  Awesome athletes / by Ron Horton.
    p. cm. — (History makers)
Summary: Profiles six athletes who participate in the extreme sports of skateboarding, snowboarding, surfing, rock climbing, mountain bike racing, and kayaking.
Includes bibliographical references and index.
  ISBN 1-59018-307-X (hardcover : alk. paper)
  1. Athletes—Biography—Juvenile literature. [1. Athletes. 2. Extreme sports.] I. Title. II. Series.
  GV697.A1H66 2004
  796'.092'2—dc22
                                                    2003013200

Printed in the United States of America

Contents

FOREWORD

The literary form most often referred to as "multiple biography" was perfected in the first century A.D. by Plutarch, a perceptive and talented moralist and historian who hailed from the small town of Chaeronea in central Greece. His most famous work, *Parallel Lives*, consists of a long series of biographies of noteworthy ancient Greek and Roman statesmen and military leaders. Frequently, Plutarch compares a famous Greek to a famous Roman, pointing out similarities in personality and achievements. These expertly constructed and very readable tracts provided later historians and others, including playwrights like Shakespeare, with priceless information about prominent ancient personages and also inspired new generations of writers to tackle the multiple biography genre.

The Lucent History Makers series proudly carries on the venerable tradition handed down from Plutarch. Each volume in the series consists of a set of five to eight biographies of important and influential historical figures who were linked together by a common factor. In *Rulers of Ancient Rome*, for example, all the figures were generals, consuls, or emperors of either the Roman Republic or Empire; while the subjects of *Fighters Against American Slavery*, though they lived in different places and times, all shared the same goal, namely the eradication of human servitude. Mindful that politicians and military leaders are not (and never have been) the only people who shape the course of history, the editors of the series have also included representatives from a wide range of endeavors, including scientists, artists, writers, philosophers, religious leaders, and sports figures.

Each book is intended to give a range of figures—some well known, others less known; some who made a great impact on history, others who made only a small impact. For instance, by making Columbus's initial voyage possible, Spain's Queen Isabella I, featured in *Women Leaders of Nations*, helped to open up the New World to exploration and exploitation by the European powers. Inarguably, therefore, she made a major contribution to a series of events that had momentous consequences for the entire world. By contrast, Catherine II, the eighteenth-century Russian queen, and Golda Meir, the modern Israeli prime minister, did not play roles of global impact; however, their policies and actions significantly influenced the historical development of both their own countries and their regional neighbors. Regardless of their relative importance in the greater historical scheme, all of the figures chronicled in the History Makers series made contributions to posterity; and their public achievements, as well as what is known about their private lives, are presented and evaluated in light of the most recent scholarship.

In addition, each volume in the series is documented and substantiated by a wide array of primary and secondary source quotations. The primary source quotes enliven the text by presenting eyewitness views of the times and culture in which each history maker lived; while the secondary source quotes, taken from the works of respected modern scholars, offer expert elaboration and/ or critical commentary. Each quote is footnoted, demonstrating to the reader exactly where biographers find their information. The footnotes also provide the reader with the means of conducting additional research. Finally, to further guide and illuminate readers, each volume in the series features photographs, two bibliographies, and a comprehensive index.

The History Makers series provides both students engaged in research and more casual readers with informative, enlightening, and entertaining overviews of individuals from a variety of circumstances, professions, and backgrounds. No doubt all of them, whether loved or hated, benevolent or cruel, constructive or destructive, will remain endlessly fascinating to each new generation seeking to identify the forces that shaped their world.

Motivation, Determination, and Innovation

Action sports such as cycling, climbing, and kayaking are different from team sports such as basketball or soccer. Action sports pit the athlete not only against an obstacle or an opponent, but also against the self. Victory in action sports relies on the individual's determination and personal training rather than team effort and expert coaching.

Competitive skateboarding, which involves one individual after another performing on a half pipe–shaped ramp, is an example of how an athlete must rely on inner resources for victory. The skater moves back and forth and executes tricks and stunts in midair by gaining speed and launching off the ramp's edge. The skater's determination not just to outdo all the other competitors but to achieve some sort of personal first can provide the necessary margin of victory. Competitive snowboarding, which also involves doing tricks on a half pipe, is similar.

In surfing competitions, the surfer balances on his board, riding the ocean's wave, carving the foam caps and spinning off of its lip, performing tricks until the ride is over. The freestyle kayaker uses the same force of water, but on a river instead of the ocean. The paddler works the kayak into a spinning, washing machine–like whirlpool and then executes a series of tricks using a paddle to position the boat. All of these four sports are similar in that victory is determined by the number of tricks the athlete performs in an allotted amount of time and the degree of skill required to execute those tricks. A point score is totaled from a series of attempts, and the participant with the highest total score wins.

Rock climbing and mountain biking differ from the other sports. In professional sport climbing, the athlete is judged on the speed and precision with which he or she climbs the route, as well as whether or not the climb is completed. Rather than performing stunts, the climber must attempt to complete more difficult routes in a shorter period of time. Points are given for these categories and a total is added from a series of climbs to determine a winner.

Mountain bike racing is the most conventional of action sports, with a standard track, generally on wooded trails. The racer starts at the beginning and must go to the end of the course. Mountain bikers must push the limitations of the body's endurance, battling fatigue while maneuvering the bicycle through rocks and tree roots on steep, narrow trails. Sometimes laps are done on a shorter course; other times one long trail serves for the entire race. In either case, the racer with the fastest time wins.

Traits of the Athletes

Athletes in any sport have in common certain traits that enable them to perform at the top of their respective games. For example, they all

A surfer charges through a massive wave barrel in Tahiti. Surfing is an action sport that pits the athlete against nature.

A pair of mountain climbers reaches the top of a challenging peak. Succeeding in action sports requires tremendous determination to overcome physical and mental obstacles.

take their sports seriously, devoting time and effort to achieve perfection. Motivation, determination, and innovation are three factors that separate awesome athletes from the merely great ones.

From an early age, an athlete who wants to reach the top must have winning as a goal. In other words, a vaguely conceived goal of excellence, while important, must be accompanied by a passion to be number one. This passion is something that transcends competence in a particular sport. Lynn Hill, for example, participated in competitive gymnastics and swimming at an early age. The lessons she learned served her well in her drive to become the top female sport climber in the world. Hill's motivation enabled her to attain any goal she set.

A professional athlete must also be determined to meet his or her goals regardless of obstacles. Those obstacles can exist in a physical form, such as a mishap during competition, or they can be mental or both. For example, when Ned Overend experienced a flat tire in the first lap of the 1988 World Mountain Bike Championship, he could have blamed the mishap on fate and chosen not to continue. The flat was less of a problem than the mental hurdle of knowing that he had lost four minutes—an eternity in his sport. Ned Overend's determination enabled him to come back and win the race as well as the world title that year.

Determination can often help an athlete overcome obstacles, but the athlete also must be innovative in order to handle the unexpected. This is particularly true in action sports which, unlike conventional sports such as football and basketball, have no referee who can blow a whistle and stop all play. In action sports, athletes must deal with a variety of circumstances as they present themselves, because there is no way to, for example, stop and reset a big wave or halt gravity's pull on an airborne body. Innovation also comes in the form of creativity, approaching the sport as it has never been thought of before. The first time Bob Burnquist dropped into a ramp switch stance, it was likely by accident. Rather than falling off and starting over in the normal fashion, he intuited that the ability to skate ramps both backward and forward would open up entirely new opportunities to excel. By making the connection, however, he not only went beyond just being another really good skateboarder but raised competitive skateboarding to a new level.

The athletes profiled in this book possess all of these traits. They excelled at sports in their youth and sought new ways to push their limits. These athletes were determined to succeed and pursue their goals, even when the odds were against them. They questioned what was considered the norm in their respective sports and explored the limits of the human body's capabilities.

The Awesome Athletes

Bob Burnquist first entered the North American skateboarding scene in 1995, performing tricks no one thought possible in a switch stance, both backwards and forwards, on his board. Throughout his competitive career, he tried more and more challenging tricks in switch stance, continuing to push the limits of possibility in vertical skateboarding.

Snowboarder Terje Haakonsen is the undisputed dominator of half pipe competition. Haakonsen mastered the art of catching major air on his board, performing a variety of twists and flips and spins with every phenomenally high jump. Choosing to lead rather than follow, he boycotted the Olympics, instead creating his own snowboard contest in his native Norway that attracts the top performers in the sport each year.

Kelly Slater's aggressive, acrobatic style of surfing forever changed ideas of what was possible with a board and a wave. He won the Association of Surfing Professionals World Champion title in 1992, and became the first person to ever win the same title five years in a row from 1994–1998.

Lynn Hill learned to climb during the free climbing revolution, setting her sights on challenging routes with incredibly difficult moves. She was the first person to ever free climb Yosemite's famous Nose route. One year later, Hill repeated the same feat in a twenty-four-hour period, exhibiting her ability to perform the most difficult moves on the most challenging routes with speed and grace.

Ned Overend is known as the father of mountain bike racing. An avid runner, cyclist, and triathlete, Overend was perfectly designed to dominate the sport. Nicknamed "the lung," Overend seemed to perform best when the terrain was at its most challenging.

Eric Jackson is one of the most versatile paddlers in the history of kayaking. Not only did he race for the U.S. slalom team, competing in World Cup and Olympic competitions, but he was also a pioneer in the sport of freestyle kayaking, winning world championship titles in both 1993 and 2001.

These six individuals used their motivation, determination, and innovation to reach the top, and in the process became truly awesome.

CHAPTER 1

Bob Burnquist: Master of the Switch Stance

In 1995, Bob Burnquist forever changed competitive skateboarding. Burnquist went from an unknown, if competent, skateboarder to a top competitor overnight with his performance at the Slam City Jam contest in Vancouver, British Columbia. Skaters had performed at high skill levels before, but Burnquist was the first to do so both backward and forward. Not only was Burnquist innovative, but he was also versatile, repeatedly raising the bar of what is possible on a skateboard with his amazing performances.

Growing Up in Brazil

Robert Dean Silva Burnquist was born in Rio de Janeiro, Brazil, on October 10, 1976. His parents, Dean and Dora, met in Brazil in the early 1970s. Dean, a native of Bakersfield, California, was working in Brazil as a coffee exporter. The couple soon married, and moved to São Paulo, Brazil. Their first child was a girl named Milena, Bob came next, and another girl, Rebecca, followed. While much of Brazil's populace are poverty stricken, the Burnquist family lived an upper-middle-class existence, with enough money for the children to attend private school.

As Burnquist grew older, he learned to play soccer, which is a passion among many in Brazil. Burnquist suffered from asthma, however, so he played goalie, because that position involved the least amount of running, which aggravated his condition. Eventually Burnquist became interested in skateboarding, and soon traded his soccer ball for his first skateboard. As he became more interested in his new sport, his father bought him all new skateboard parts for his eleventh birthday and the two assembled the present together. That same year, a skateboard park called Ultra opened near his house, and Burnquist became a regular visitor there.

Skateboarding became Burnquist's favorite activity, to the point that he skipped school regularly to skateboard. Since he always made it home at noon, the time when school normally recessed for lunch,

Burnquist's parents were slow to find out about his truancy. When school officials finally called because Burnquist had missed so many classes, his parents punished him by taking his skateboard away. That made little difference because Burnquist simply borrowed a board and continued with his routine. All of this time and devotion to the sport, coupled with a natural athletic ability and sense of balance, made Burnquist a highly skilled skateboarder.

A Difficult Choice

Eventually the skate park near his house closed, but that did not discourage Burnquist, who switched to street skating. The abundance

Brazilian Bob Burnquist left his native country as a teenager to pursue a career in the United States as a professional skateboarder.

of pedestrians and traffic on Brazilian streets, however, made skateboarding difficult. Burnquist often spent more time searching for a place to skate than he did actually skateboarding. Spending time on the streets of São Paulo had a negative effect on the young skater. There, he was exposed to a culture of which using drugs was an integral part. Burnquist began experimenting with activities such as sniffing glue and other inhalants that were popular among the street people of São Paulo.

Burnquist recalls his early experience with drugs: "I . . . started . . . hanging out with older people, and kind of strayed away a little bit." He goes on to say that his love of skateboarding saved him from drugs and a life on the streets: "Skateboarding was always there, so I had to make a choice—either skateboarding or the other road . . . drugs are pretty hard to get out of if you don't have a strong will. If you have something that you love, you can go anywhere."[1] Burnquist's love was his sport, and he turned away from drugs and fully concentrated on perfecting his skateboarding technique.

Technique was important for Burnquist, since he was inclined to take chances, and the concrete and metal of São Paulo's streets and skate parks were unforgiving. Experiencing mishaps on a regular basis due to his aggressive skating style, Burnquist often walked to the hospital with broken bones, concussions, and contusions, then called his parents for a ride home after he was treated. By his own estimates over the years, Burnquist suffered roughly fifteen broken bones, some, such as his wrist, on multiple occasions. Upon returning from treatment, the casts on his injured limbs never lasted long. As soon as he felt the least bit better, the young skater would cut them off and return to skating.

Burnquist Masters Two Skating Styles

The sport for which Burnquist had developed such an obsession is generally broken into two categories, street skating and vert, short for vertical, skating. Street skaters perform their sport in the open terrain of the city on stair rails, curbs, and benches, using natural gaps as springboards for their jumps and tricks. Vert skating includes similar jumps and tricks performed on a high-walled plywood or cement ramp shaped like half of a pipe. Burnquist's command of both street and vert skating was unusual, since most skaters concentrate on one category or the other. His diversity enabled him to mix elements from both disciplines to form his signature style.

As Burnquist became more proficient, he began entering competitions. He experienced some success in these contests and as a result considered turning professional. That decision, as it turned out, was almost accidental, since unlike American skateboarding, induction into the ranks of Brazilian professionals was rather informal. Burnquist recalls the day in 1991 when he became a professional, explaining "I turned pro when I was fourteen. There was a pro contest, and I qualified first for the finals. . . . I just told the guy announcing that I was pro. He announced, 'we got a new pro.'" [2]

Although his pro skateboarding debut was rather anticlimactic in that he did not win, Burnquist continued to enter professional events throughout Brazil in the following years, gaining both competitive insight and skill in the process. The skater's innovative style caught the attention of Brazilian skate company sponsors like Momento Angular, Slide, and Urgh. Corporate sponsorship did not mean Bob would be paid, but now his clothing, gear, and entry fees to contests were covered. This early support enabled Bob to compete more, gaining both experience and exposure in the process.

Burnquist's Skateboarding Style

Learning to skate in Brazil gave Burnquist the edge he needed to succeed over many of his future competitors. Writer Alec Wilkinson describes Burnquist as a

> fearless, supple and apparently effortless skater. He also skates very fast. His aggressiveness derives from his having grown up skating on cement. You land wrong on cement and you're taking no less than the rest of the day off. American skaters learn to skate on wooden ramps. To Burnquist, falling on wood is generally a matter of indifference. [3]

Burnquist is most famous for his ability to ride "switch stance" or backwards on his board. Most people ride in one direction, with either their right foot ("normal") or their left foot ("goofy") at the back of the board. Burnquist proved himself virtually ambidextrous on a board, performing stunts no other skater would dream of doing, in any direction he chose. This multidirectional style of skateboarding had never been practiced in competition before Burnquist's arrival on the professional scene.

Burnquist Enters the Spotlight

Another way Burnquist changed skateboarding was simply by drawing the skating world's attention to Brazilian skaters, who had been largely ignored outside their home country. In 1994, Jake Phelps, editor of *Thrasher,* one of the most popular U.S. skate magazines, came to Brazil with some other skateboarders to write an article on the country's skate scene. As a result of Burnquist's ability to speak both

English and Brazil's national language, Portuguese, he was a natural choice for a guide. The Americans got a chance to see the skater in action, and were impressed with his command of the sport. The magazine representatives encouraged him to tour the United States. Within the year Burnquist visited California, spending a month exploring the American skate scene. During his travels he met fellow skater Jen O'Brien in Lake Tahoe and the two became close friends, staying in touch upon his return to Brazil.

In 1995, Burnquist came north once again, this time to Canada. With the encouragement of Phelps, Burnquist entered his first international pro skateboard contest, the Slam City Jam, in Vancouver,

Burnquist completes a frontside air at a skatepark in Marseilles, France. Burnquist grew up skating on cement ramps instead of the wooden ones common in the United States.

British Columbia. This event was typical of skateboarding competitions, which generally consist of a forty-five-second qualifying run in which the skater links together a series of complex tricks, jumps, and flips on the board. Each of these stunts is given a point status by a panel of judges. If the participant's run qualifies, he then moves on to a one-minute run on the same course.

Burnquist recalls his experience at the Slam City Jam:

> One of my sponsors helped pay for my ticket. I didn't expect much. I just wanted to have a good time. I'd skate half the run, then stop and go switch. I remember people in the stands going, "Switch! Switch!" . . . . So then I put two and two together: If I expanded on skating switch stance, I could progress skateboarding in a way that hadn't been approached before. . . . I skated the finals. . . . I won. That contest was the turning point. Things started happening after that.[4]

After the competition, the American skateboard company Anti-Hero immediately signed on to sponsor Burnquist and put out a board with his name and an artistic design of his choice on it. Unlike his early Brazilian sponsors, Anti-Hero issued Burnquist a paycheck in addition to taking care of his travel expenses and entry fees for competitions. Although he had been a sponsored skateboarder and had been competing in Brazil since 1989, it took success in the United States and international press coverage to enable him to support himself solely through skateboarding. He describes his feelings of the sponsorship, declaring, "Finally, I was able to live off skateboarding, and then I really considered myself a pro skateboarder."[5]

Professional Touring and Media Coverage

Following the Slam City Jam, Burnquist returned to Brazil, although he had no intention of staying. His sole purpose in returning was to get his high school diploma before moving to the United States. Since his father was a U.S. citizen, Burnquist had citizenship in both countries. Burnquist's plan to fulfill his country's high school equivalency program, however, required that he pass numerous tests, which left him frustrated. Burnquist decided to move to the States without graduating. He settled in Daly City, California, where he soon earned his General Equivalency Diploma (GED).

Burnquist began touring the United States and competing professionally in a variety of skateboarding contests. Competing regularly in the summer X-Games, Burnquist's name became inextricably linked with the future of the sport. Not only was he a newcomer to the competitive circuit, but his flair for innovation and raw talent propelled professional skating to higher levels. Even professionals who had competed for years were stunned by the prospect of performing such demanding tricks in switch stance.

As a result of his contributions to the direction of professional skateboarding, *Thrasher* magazine named Burnquist Skater of the Year for 1997. Also, in a poll of his peers in *Transworld Skateboarding* magazine, Burnquist was voted best vert skater in both 1998 and 1999. Not only did skateboarders consider him an amazing athlete, but *Rolling Stone* magazine named him one of their athletes of the year for 1999 in the category of alternative sports.

During this period, Burnquist continued to tour and compete. He describes his experience, stating "The best thing about traveling is the people you get to meet and the different life spectrums you witness. When you realize how many different cultures and lives are lived throughout the world, it's the most humbling experience." He adds, "You can't just receive the pleasure in traveling without paying a little, too. Sometimes it gets stressful when you have responsibilities and the trip is . . . full of physical activities . . . you get to your destination and have to rip under the scrutiny of the crowd and the pressure of expectancy, I'd rather be a lot of places other than right there."[6]

Traveling on the pro-skate circuit had many stresses, but it also gave Burnquist a chance to see more of the world and meet new and interesting people. During his travels in 1998 Burnquist reconnected with pro skater Jen O'Brien, and the two began dating. Burnquist describes the nature of their relationship: "Jen O'Brien is teaching me about love and relationships with a great friendship. She is definitely the most influential [person] in my life right now."[7]

Focusing on Family and Health

In April of 2000, Jen and Bob became parents when Lotus O'Brien Silva Burnquist was born. With the addition of a child to his life, Burnquist began focusing on creating an environment in which he could raise a family. The couple moved south to the California town of Vista, just north of San Diego, and bought a large tract of land. Bob, Jen, and Lotus moved into one house on the property, and Burnquist invited his mother, Dora, to live in another house on the same property. Meanwhile, his father Dean stayed in Brazil to run his coffee export business. He explained his motives at the time as a ". . . need to be more focused for Lotus and Jen . . . for my family. It's quite a change. There's a lot more to it now."[8] Burnquist did, however, make sure that he would have ample opportunities to spend time with fellow skateboarders by building a large skate ramp in his backyard.

Winning several contests as a professional skateboarder enabled Burnquist to support himself and his family without difficulty. Rather than spending money supporting a lavish lifestyle, Bob was conservative with his newfound wealth, putting much of his winnings in savings. He also looked toward his future, when he would not be able to earn a living as a competitive skateboarder, while giving something of himself back to the community. With his earnings, Burnquist started a company called Burnquist Organics that sold produce on a farm adjacent to his house in Vista. Burnquist's father Dean moved to California as well, and he took charge of the farm's production.

In addition to this agricultural endeavor, Burnquist also opened up a restaurant called Melodia, which is Portuguese for melody, in the nearby beach community of Leucadia. Melodia served Brazilian dishes made from all organically grown produce from his farm and fresh seafood. Bob's older sister, Milena, helped manage the restaurant, and his mother served as the head chef, using her family recipes and lifelong knowledge of Brazilian cuisine. Having his entire immediate family nearby gave Burnquist a sense of balance in what continued to be a hectic travel and competition schedule.

Burnquist's main interest in promoting healthy food was directly linked to his observations of the young people he met as he traveled to skateboarding competitions. Bob noticed how unhealthy and overweight so many of them were as a result of their high-fat diets of fast foods. He explains that as a role model for teens, he has a responsibility to set a good example:

> There's a solution to [teens' unhealthy lifestyles], and it lies with the professional athletes of the world. These kids are looking up to Kobe Bryant endorsing McDonald's. You see all these studies about how fat kids are, and obesity levels are the highest ever now. With this restaurant, I feel like I'm sending out a good message. . . . I'm trying to do something here with what I have. I was handed all these blessings, and now I gotta give it back somehow.[9]

Remaining true to his ideals, Burnquist refused sponsorship from any company that promoted what he considered an unhealthy lifestyle.

Expanding Skill and Fame

Burnquist continued to win in vert skateboard competitions around the world. In 2000, he switched his major sponsorship from Anti-

Burnquist launches a Japan air at a famous cement half pipe near São Paulo, Brazil. Burnquist relishes being a positive role model for Brazilian youth.

Hero to a company called The Firm, run by fellow skater Lance Mountain. That same year, he took first place in the renowned Vans Triple Crown, a feat that he repeated in 2001. Other competitors found it hard to beat the young Brazilian who could perform the same tricks they did—full body spins, flips, and twists—both backward and forward on his board. At the 2001 Tampa Pro, Burnquist once again proved he was master of his sport by completing a full plywood loop, similar to that of a roller coaster, both regular and switch stance. Executing a full loop on a board is a feat that few skaters have mastered, but the ability to perform it both backward and forward belongs to Burnquist alone.

Constantly wishing to push the level at which he performs, Burnquist decided to make the full loop even more difficult by removing one of the top plywood sections. This missing section requires the skater to jump the newly created gap upside down in midair. In June of 2002, Burnquist successfully completed this full loop with the top removed at the OP King of Skate competition held in Los Angeles. The event was broadcast on pay-per-view television, reaching audiences around the globe. For his contributions to the sport of skateboarding, Burnquist was awarded the Laureus World Alternative Sportsperson of the Year award in 2002.

Playing Video Games and Skating with Monkeys

While much of Burnquist's fame was among die-hard skateboarding fans who watched his performances in competitions, his renown became more mainstream through movies and video games. Aside from the numerous appearances in skate industry videos, Burnquist appeared in two feature movies, both filmed in his own backyard. The first movie was an ESPN-sponsored film *Ultimate X*, an IMAX film featuring Bob performing stunts on his backyard ramp.

The next film, *Most Vertical Primate 2*, was a more fantasy-oriented children's movie about a talented monkey named Jack who quits playing professional hockey and begins a career as a skateboarder. The film involved a scene in which Burnquist and the monkey skateboard together on his home ramp. Bob expresses his feelings on mainstream movies that include skateboarding, explaining, "A lot of good can come out of these bigger movie productions that don't necessarily focus on skateboarding only. . . . Even if it's just kind of scratching the surface, it's giving us an opportunity to show skateboarding. . . . Suddenly people watch it and get excited . . . and get interested in skateboarding. . . . I think it was a great experience." [10]

Another way that Burnquist sought to touch the lives of non-skaters was through video games. He was a featured skater in Tony Hawk's Pro Skater video game. In addition, the game's creator, Activision, signed a deal with Burnquist to promote his own video game in the future. Will Kassoy, the vice president of Activision, states, "Bob is one of the most popular and respected athletes in action sports today. Throughout his career he has been an inspiration for thousands of up and coming skaters in the world. We are very pleased to extend our relationship in video games with Bob, and are excited to have Bob as an Activision sponsored athlete." [11] Along with this deal came a series of action figures and trading cards featuring both Burnquist and other professional skaters portrayed in the video game. Through this medium, Burnquist reached an audience that may never have actually ridden a skateboard.

Bob's Skateboarding Future

While skateboarding has been Burnquist's main focus for nearly fifteen years, it is not his only interest. He also snowboards and surfs, feeling as if participating in the three board sports ensures his ability to be active anywhere, any time of the year. He also enjoys photography and music, taking his camera and guitar on every tour and vacation. These interests, as well as his focus on family and healthy living, make him a diverse role model not only for skateboarders,

Bob Burnquist (second from right) poses with fellow Brazilian skateboarders. Burnquist's success has helped other Brazilian skaters gain recognition.

but everyone. Although his restaurant, Melodia, closed its doors at the end of 2002, Burnquist Organics is still in full production mode, growing fruits and vegetables without the use of chemical fertilizers or pesticides.

Burnquist realizes that his future as a pro skater is limited by his body's ability to perform. He acknowledges that his age, health, and ability to recover from injury will ultimately limit his longevity as a professional athlete. Time spent traveling also weighs on his motivation to perform, but he treats skateboarding like a job that enables him to put healthful food on his table and support his family, making skateboarding both Burnquist's job and his passion. He explains, "Skateboarding gives me direction. It gives me motivation to live. I just know that with skateboarding I can accomplish anything I set my mind to. It's a way to express myself, an outlet to release what I feel." [12]

In 2003, Burnquist toured his native Brazil. Skateboarding, he says, had such a positive influence on his youth that he wanted to share his experience and support other young skaters in their endeavors. Although he plans to stay in the United States, Burnquist feels a responsibility to his native land. He explains:

> It's important for kids in Brazil to have someone to look up to. This is the first time a pro or a skateboarder from down there has come to the States, traveled everywhere, and is in the magazines and such. . . . When I go back there, kids are really supportive . . . and they look up to me. I have to make sure I don't lead them in the wrong way. It's a big responsibility I have. [13]

CHAPTER 2

Terje Haakonsen: King of the Half Pipe

Ask almost any snowboarder who best represents their sport as the top athlete and the reply will most certainly be Terje Haakonsen. The native Norwegian took the sport of half pipe snowboarding to levels never imagined. Haakonsen has shown that he can ride faster, jump higher, and perform more incredible tricks on a snowboard than any other athlete in the history of the sport. Unwilling to compromise his ideals about where the sport of snowboarding was headed, Haakonsen took an active role in creating new competitions and ensuring that control of his sport remained in the hands of the athletes who participated in it. Not only was he the world's best half pipe snowboarder, but he was also a true spokesperson for the sport as a whole.

A Natural Born Athlete

Terje Haakonsen was born on October 11, 1974, on the island of Soroya, just off the coast of the northern Norwegian state of Finnmark, where he spent the first few years of his life. When Terje was five, the Haakonsens moved to the Telemark village of Amot, about thirty miles east of Oslo. Terje's father was a hotel chef and his mother was a special education teacher. The family lived a comfortable life in a region that was world famous for skiing. Taking advantage of what their new surroundings had to offer, Terje and his brother built ski jumps out of the massive amounts of snow that fell each year. These experiences marked the beginning of an ongoing love affair with snow, as Terje learned how to throw himself into the air on skis, performing airborne spins and jumps with precision.

As a child, Haakonsen participated in a variety of sports, but his favorites, in addition to skiing, were skateboarding and soccer. Even at a very young age, he could run at top speed, throwing himself into a flip that would provide the momentum necessary to propel the soccer ball thirty yards down the sideline. In fact, he was one of the fastest runners on the team, dominating his opponents in the midfield position. Haakonsen came by such speed naturally; he recalls his father, Per, dropping by practice and outrunning the kids, even though he was still dressed in his work clothes. To this day, Haakonsen wonders how far he could have gone professionally if he had continued to play soccer.

The Grooming of a Champion

Haakonsen had been an avid skier for eight years when, at the age of thirteen, he jumped at the chance to try a new snow sport, one that resembled the skateboarding he enjoyed. Instead of wheels, the board featured a flat, waxed surface with metal edges like skis that allowed its rider to jump obstacles, carve steep waves of snow, and execute tricks, spins, and flips on every turn. Haakonsen borrowed a neighbor's snowboard and was immediately hooked. He enumerates the reasons he took to the snowboard so quickly: "You could do so many more tricks on it than on skis. You had no sticks in your hand, and you used the terrain way better. It was more like surfing." [14]

Shortly after his first snowboarding experience, Haakonsen began saving the money he earned cutting grass and sorting mail at the hotel where his father worked to purchase his first board. He began exploring a wide variety of terrain, from steep, powdered slopes to moguls and slopes with natural obstacles such as rocks and trees. Haakonsen's natural ability on the snowboard soon gained the attention of Einhar Loftus, a professional snowboarder also from Telemark. Loftus took Haakonsen as his protégé and showed him not only how to refine his technique, but also the intricacies of competition. One major skill that Loftus imparted to Haakonsen was how to "catch big air"—that is, execute high jumps—on a board. The ability to perform this maneuver on a board is critical to a competitive snowboarder. In order to execute the tricks on which they are judged, snowboarders need plenty of clearance between themselves and the ground. With his already highly developed balance and agility, Haakonsen excelled at gaining "big air" and pulling off a wide array of moves on each jump.

Drawn to the Half Pipe

Haakonsen was naturally drawn to freestyle snowboarding, which combined his desire to perform stunts on his board with his natural talent of catching air. Soon after his initiation to snowboarding, Haakonsen began entering freestyle competitions. During these contests, he would race down the 350-foot-long, U-shaped ramp, jumping his board off of the ten-foot-high walls. With every launch off the half pipe's lip, he could twist, spin, and flip on his board.

Although he had only been boarding for two years, with Loftus's encouragement and mentoring, Haakonsen was able to enter the world championships at age fifteen in 1990. In the competition the young boy went from relative obscurity to worldwide popularity as he placed fifth that year. In 1992, Haakonsen won both the U.S. Open and the European championships for freestyle half pipe competition.

Norwegian Terje Haakonsen awaits his next half pipe run. Haakonsen was drawn to the sport of snowboarding because it incorporates elements from surfing, skiing, and skateboarding.

One trait that Haakonsen became known for in his early career was his use of new, unrehearsed tricks in competition. In a sport in which one fall results in disqualification, most riders stick to a proven, point-winning routine, but Haakonsen did not let fear of failure hold him back from exploring the boundaries of his ability. He explains. "For me, it's not that important to count points. I don't need to win titles or be number one. I just need to please myself." [15] His desire to push for the hardest moves in competition won Haakonsen the respect and admiration of supporters, rivals, and more important in advancing his career, judges.

Dominating the Half Pipe

Terje Haakonsen continued to exhibit his mastery of the sport with European championship wins in 1993 and 1994, U.S. Open wins in 1993 and 1995, and World Snowboard Championship wins in 1994 and 1995. Haakonsen became the most recognized face in the half pipe competition and he was praised as the most talented snowboarder in the history of the sport. Fellow snowboarder and snowboarding equipment company owner Jake Burton describes Haakonsen: "He's got phenomenal athleticism and creativity. . . . And his moves are usually the biggest, usually the most technically difficult, and the cleanest. His influence has been immense. Before Haakonsen, people never dreamed they could go that high." [16]

Some of the moves that Haakonsen performs in the half pipe are multiple 360-degree turns and both front and back flips. Variations on these moves include the Cabalerial, which is a 360-degree full rotation starting from a backward, or fakey, riding stance. Another move, the McTwist, involves a 540-degree rotation of one-and-a-half turns combined with a backflip. While these moves seem dangerous and unbelievable enough on their own, Haakonsen went even one step further in forming his signature move, the Haakon Flip. This move consists of launching out of the half pipe and executing a flip with two full spins (720 degrees) of his board. Pro snowboarder Todd Richards describes Terje's ability: "Depending on his moods, Haakonsen will put in the most amazing runs. He does what he wants to, when he wants to, knowing he can win whenever he wants to." [17]

Tropical Vacation for the Family

By 1996, Haakonsen was able to support himself with money earned from competition and product endorsements. During snowboarding's off season that year, Haakonsen lived in Mililani, Hawaii. This time served as a break from snowboarding, giving Haakonsen a

Haakonsen launches a method air at the 2002 X-Games in Aspen, Colorado. Haakonsen dominated most professional half pipe events throughout the 1990s.

chance to relax from his strenuous travel and competition schedule. While he claimed to not train at all for boarding during these times, activities such as surfing and skateboarding kept him in relatively good shape year-round. It was during his stay in Hawaii that Haakonsen became a father. His son Michael was born in 1997. The boy would spend part of the year in Hawaii with his mother, and the other part with Terje Haakonsen at one of his various residences in Norway and the United States.

A Contest by Boarders for Boarders

Although Haakonsen was best known for his domination of half pipe events, his versatility allowed him to excel at all aspects of the sport. For example, the Mount Baker Banked Slalom, a contest held in the Cascade Mountains of Washington state, is one of the most highly respected events in the sport. This slalom race differs from half pipe competition in that competitors race down a plotted course, weaving through flags, in an attempt to score the fastest time.

Fellow Banked Slalom competitor Dave Sypniewski describes the significance of the event: "It's fitting that the race is held every year on Super Bowl Sunday, because . . . it is of equal comparison. It has the same significance . . . as the NBA championships, the World Series, the Final Four, and the Stanley Cup. . . . A person who wins such as Terje, should be compared to Michael Jordan." [18] Winning the Mount Baker Banked Slalom is such an accomplishment among snowboarders because it represents a boarder-designed and regulated competition that involves little of the corporate and media hype that plagues most other contests.

Haakonsen boycotted the Winter Olympics of 1998. His refusal to compete shocked the world of professional snowboarding.

Over the next six years, Haakonsen won this event four times. On one occasion, having achieved the fastest time in his first qualifying run down the course and confident of his ability, Haakonsen pulled off one of the boldest displays of talent on his next run. He rode the entire course backward or fakey. Sportswriter Franz Lidz describes this feat as "roughly the equivalent of [San Francisco 49ers quarterback] Steve Young's throwing three touchdown passes lefty and then, out of boredom, heaving a fourth right handed."[19] If it was unclear to anyone in the snowboarding community just how talented Haakonsen actually is, his performances at Mount Baker confirmed his abilities.

1998 Olympic Boycott

While Terje Haakonsen gained fame for his natural ability and competitive spirit, it was for a single decision not to join a competition that he gained notoriety. In 1998, when snowboarding was introduced to the Winter Olympics, Haakonsen boycotted the Games, which were held in Nagano, Japan. The controversy arose when the International Olympic Committee (IOC), considering snowboarding to be an offshoot of downhill skiing, placed the Federation Internationale du Ski (FIS) in charge of the snowboarding event. Most professional snowboarders, including Haakonsen, were members of the International Snowboarding Federation and felt that their organization should oversee the competition. They were outraged at the IOC's decision.

Haakonsen had two major objections to the FIS controlling the Olympic snowboarding event. The first objection was with how the FIS structured the competition. Snowboarders would be allowed only two runs instead of the six to eight runs they were accustomed to. Haakonsen expressed his views on the subject to Franz Lidz. "Having only two [runs] is boring for the spectators and means a lot of sitting around for the competitors. With more runs the action doesn't stop, and the riders get to show more of their stuff."[20]

Haakonsen's second complaint against the IOC's decision related to suspicions regarding the motives of the FIS. With its decision to put the FIS in charge of the Olympic event, Haakonsen felt the OIC was allowing the ski industry, which was heavily represented in the FIS, to take over snowboarding. The FIS's sudden interest in snowboarding seemed odd, in light of the fact that for years snowboarders had looked for support from the skiing community to no avail.

In addition to their other concerns, many snowboarders were concerned by corporate sponsorship of the Olympics. Rather than wearing the clothes they felt comfortable in, bearing logos of companies that had sponsored them for years, participants were expected to wear multicolored uniforms bearing the logos of official Olympic sponsors. To accede to such a requirement, Haakonsen and others felt, would be a slap in the face to longtime supporters. In general, many snowboarders including Haakonsen considered the IOC's decision a blatant disregard for the history and preexisting culture of snowboarding.

Beyond the implications for his sport of the IOC's decision, Haakonsen objected to the commercialism and chauvinism that had become hallmarks of the Olympics. He describes his thoughts on the subject:

> Snowboarding is about fresh tracks and carving powder and being yourself and not being judged by others. . . . It's not about nationalism, politics, and big money. . . . I'm not going to run around waving a flag . . . I don't ride for my country. . . . American riders are more into the whole Olympic thing. Personally, I think it's not a big deal. . . . Snowboarding is everything the Olympics isn't. I don't really want to be part of them.[21]

Criticism and Support Behind the Boycott

Haakonsen's decision to boycott the 1998 Olympic Games was greeted with both support and criticism. The Norwegian snowboard federation and the majority of his sponsors, with the exception of Burton Snowboards, put immense pressure on Haakonsen to compete in the Games. His peers and fellow snowboarders were divided. Some felt he should compete, but refuse to accept the medals if he won. Others supported him fully, on the grounds that only an athlete as talented as Haakonsen could make his voice heard and loosen the FIS's hold on the sport.

For his part, Haakonsen explains his choice to not compete in the 1998 Games: "If I came and threw the medal in the river, it doesn't really matter because I went and supported the gig. It would go in one ear and out the other. A lot of close friends wanted me to go. They said, 'You're going to regret it in 20 years.' I didn't struggle with this decision. It's rational, not emotional."[22] Many would-be competitors felt that Haakonsen's absence cheated them of their chance to truly win the gold. Most snowboarders realized that in the world's best snowboarder's absence, they were actually only competing amongst themselves for second place.

Terje Haakonsen

Bob Burnquist

Lynn Hill

Kelly Slater

Ned Overend

Eric Jackson

Bob Burnquist

Terje Haakonsen

Lynn Hill

Kelly Slater

Ned Overend

Eric Jackson

Terje Haakonsen

Kelly Slater

Bob Burnquist

Eric Jackson

No Longer Pushing the Limits

Terje Haakonsen put the controversy over the 1998 Olympics behind him and continued to compete in International Snowboard Federation–sponsored events, winning time and time again. To observers, however, something inside Haakonsen seemed to have changed. In the years following his decision to boycott the Olympics, his emphasis had shifted from bold creativity in competition to a reliance on practiced, point-earning tricks—a change some fellow snowboarders found disappointing. Haakonsen acknowledged that his approach to the sport had softened, saying, "I'm not taking as many chances . . . I've gotten more routine, especially on the pipe. I'm doing the same tricks over and over again." He goes on to voice his rationale for his newfound conservatism: "I do have to look at this as a business. I have to protect myself. Do what's right for me. A lot of people . . . bring me different projects. And if it's a good enough concept or it's worth it to me financially, I do it. I guess I'm a sellout." [23]

Giving the Power Back to Snowboarders

As a means of breaking out of the competitive doldrums, Haakonsen invented a different kind of contest, one that would remain true to the snowboarding community—following their own format with their own sponsors. This change came in 1999 with the creation of a competition in his native country called the Arctic Challenge. This week-long event would take place in the Arctic Circle on the island of Lofoten just off the coast of Norway. The base town, Stamsund, is a traditional fishing village, and the participants would stay in coastal cabins that had for centuries been used by local fishermen. The event would bring together a small, hand-picked group of the world's top snowboarders. The purpose was to make competitors feel as comfortable as possible, so that they could perform at their peak ability. With a selective guest list, limited sponsorship, and unobtrusive media coverage, the Arctic Challenge provided serious snowboarders a haven from what Haakonsen considered overly commercialized events, especially the Olympics.

Co-organizer and fellow Norwegian, Daniel Franck, describes the event. "The Arctic Challenge is the start of a totally new contest format . . . from peer judging to timing systems, [it] will give the riders maximum scores for self-expression. We will give professional riders what they deserve, something to remember, a happening that's worth going to. The Arctic Challenge places snowboarding performance where it belongs, in the heart of its environment." [24]

Professional snowboarder and Arctic Challenge participant Peter Leines explains his views of the competition. "I was happy to go to an event put together by the riders for the riders. When snowboarders are involved with a snowboard contest, the event is going to run exactly how it should. Events like Daniel's and Terje's should happen more." [25] Haakonsen's organization of the event reminded both critics and supporters alike what creativity and power he possessed, on and off the slopes.

The Fall of the International Snowboarding Federation

The passage of time failed to change Haakonsen's opinion of the Olympics. In 2002, Haakonsen boycotted the Games in Salt Lake City, Utah. On the day the snowboarding competition was held, he was hundreds of miles away, visiting Disneyland with his four-year-old son. Just as had happened in the 1998 Games, the FIS was inflexible in dictating the event's format and refused to listen to suggestions from the snowboarding community. Protesting what they saw as the FIS's blatant disregard for snowboarders' wishes, many top competitors followed Haakonsen's earlier footsteps and boycotted the event.

Meanwhile, snowboarders had organizational problems of their own. The International Snowboarding Federation, the sport's main governing body since 1990, ceased operation in 2002. With no official organization to oversee competition, snowboarding was officially classified as a subcategory of skiing. Simply boycotting FIS-sanctioned events would no longer ensure snowboarding's independence.

With the loss of their governing body, riders needed to band together to take control of their sport again. Haakonsen's Arctic Challenge served as a model for future competitions. With the help of supportive companies such as Quiksilver, Burton, and Vans, professional snowboarders created a series of worldwide contests. The winners of these events secured a spot in Haakonsen's year-end Arctic Challenge. The qualifying competitions included the U.S Open and the European Open, along with other snowboard-friendly, corporate-sponsored events. Largely due to Haakonsen's efforts, professional snowboarders and their sponsors maintained control of their sport even though they had lost the battle over who controlled the Olympic snowboarding competition.

Haakonsen's Return to the Spirit of Snowboarding

In the years following the advent of the Arctic Challenge, Haakonsen remained an active participant and voice in the snowboarding community. He was still considered one of the greatest, if not the best snowboarder in history. Video footage of Haakonsen graced a multitude of snowboarding videos, including the IMAX production of action sports director John Long's *EXTREME*. This film shows

Haakonsen soars across a gap during a Norwegian free-riding session. Although he has reduced the number of events in which he competes, Haakonsen remains a snowboarding icon.

Haakonsen and three other professional snowboarders descending extremely steep mountain slopes surrounding Juneau, Alaska, after a storm that left ten feet of snow. Two videos by director Dave Seaone, *Subjekt Haakonsen—Life and Times of a Sprocking Cat,* and *The Haakonsen Faktor* focus almost entirely on Haakonsen. They feature a mixture of clips from childhood home movies, interviews, and snowboarding on a variety of terrain from half pipe to backcountry.

Haakonsen continues to compete in events he feels support the true spirit of snowboarding. He describes his views on competition and life:

> I don't care about just winning contests, doing what I know will win. I feel like going back to more tricks, going back to taking chances. I feel like trying more new things, taking a different line through life. I want to get that feeling again, of being a kid in the backyard, of making a jump, of doing this because this is exactly what I want to be doing.[26]

CHAPTER 3

Kelly Slater: World Champion Surfer

Kelly Slater sat in the lineup of surfers, bobbing in the waves off the Hawaiian island of Oahu's North Shore. It was February 2002, and though the surf was slightly erratic, it still produced waves up to ten feet for the surfers to carve their boards against. This was the year that Slater planned to come out of a three-and-a-half-year semiretirement to reclaim his title as the Association of Surfing Professional's top-ranked surfer. Austin Murphy described this exciting scene:

> A nice set finally rolls in, and a muscular, skin headed guy pops up. There's no question who this is . . . Slater on the board remains his sport's equivalent of Tiger [Woods] in the tee box, [hockey's Wayne] Gretzky in front of the goalmouth. . . . With a violent snap he turns, throws up a corona of spray. Now, gathering speed, he works his way onto the whitewater lip. There, for an astounding forty yards . . . he hovers along the lip, the fins of his board finding purchase where there can't possibly be any. Slater then air-drops four feet to the base of the wave, sticks the landing, and milks a few more seconds out of the ride.[27]

As the spectators looked on in disbelief and awe, there was no question whether Slater had a shot at winning the world championships for a seventh time in his career, making him arguably the greatest surfer of all time.

Early Years at the Beach

Kelly Slater was born to parents Stephen and Judy on February 11, 1972. Judy Slater was a firefighter and Steve Slater owned a bait and tackle business. Growing up in the oceanside community of Cocoa Beach, Florida, the Slater family was naturally drawn to the sea. Kelly and his older brother, Sean, spent endless hours exploring the Florida shore near their father's shop. Kelly Slater was only five when he began surfing with his brother on boards their father bought them. Kelly's natural talent on the waves became obvious when, within his first few years at the sport, he entered and won the Salick Brothers' National Kidney Foundation Event, a surfing contest held in his hometown.

Slater proved a natural athlete and participated in standard team sports such as basketball, football, and baseball. In fact, at a young age, Kelly displayed considerable talent as a pitcher. In Little League, he displayed such power that parents and opposing coaches complained he threw too fast for the kids at bat. Despite his obvious promise as a baseball player, surfing was Kelly's top priority, and he would often miss baseball practice if the waves were good. Frustrated by complaints from parents and opponents about his skill and desiring to explore his own physical limits, Slater quit team sports altogether. With the support of his parents, Slater devoted himself to surfing. Unlike his human opponents, the waves could not complain about how aggressively he threw himself at them.

Escaping into the Surf

Slater recalls that much of his passion for surfing also came out of a desire to escape from a home life made difficult by his father's alcoholism and the resulting conflict between his parents. Slater also notes that his father's alcoholism made him a strong opponent of drugs and alcohol: "Surfing was good to me for a long time. It took me away from my parents fighting constantly and getting divorced when I was eleven and from my anger at my dad. He drank a lot. . . . I was lucky—a lot of people get addicted to pills, but I got addicted to surfing. Both are escapes."[28]

After Slater's parents separated, Judy Slater was left to raise Sean, Kelly, and her youngest son, Stephen Jr., on her own. She quit her full-time job as a firefighter and worked a series of odd jobs as a bartender, emergency medical technician, and computer operator, among others. Judy was always ready to support her boys and their needs in any way that she could. In fact she landed one of her jobs as a short-order cook in order to pay off the tab that her sons had run up in the coastal restaurant, the Islander Hut, after their surf sessions. The family moved to a variety of rental homes but eventually Judy was able to put together the down payment to purchase a beach house. Luckily, all of these moves were within the community of Cocoa Beach, so the boys never had to change schools.

Meanwhile, Slater continued to surf on a daily basis. His talent was such that he excelled at moves that none of his peers could replicate. A natural competitor, Slater began traveling the East Coast a great deal during this time period, entering various surf competitions. He had to focus to maintain a balance between practice, travel, and school.

At just eighteen years old, Kelly Slater began to surf in competitions around the globe, quickly becoming one of the world's top professional surfers.

Honing Skills on Small Waves

Early on, Kelly Slater developed an acrobatic style that made his surfing distinctive. A wave was not merely a means of propelling himself and his board, but a springboard for tricks. He would double back on the wall of water, spin 360-degree turns on its crest, and shoot off of the top into midair spins, ducks, and turns. Most surfers would only attempt these moves in practice, but Slater used them in competition to win.

Unorthodox style combined with raw talent led to his rapid success. In 1982, at the age of ten, Slater won the East Coast surfing title for his age group, making him the most successful competitor on the entire eastern seaboard. He would win the same title again and again over the next five years, from 1983–1987. Two years after capturing his first East Coast title, Slater won his first of four consecutive U.S. titles, meaning that he was the best competitive surfer of his age group in the entire country.

By the age of fourteen, Slater was at the top of his sport, and soon he began to benefit from his fame. About this time, he met promoter Bryan Taylor, who began serving as his agent. While business was slow at first, Taylor knew he had a marketable resource in Slater. Taylor negotiated deals for Slater that involved modeling for clothing designers Gianni Versace and Bruno Weber, and he landed the young surfer small roles in movies and television commercials as well.

Entering the World Surf Circuit

As his skill progressed and he outgrew the relatively small waves of the eastern United States, Slater began to enter more prestigious world competitions, traveling with his older brother Sean to a variety of famous surfing destinations. His world rank among surfers went from number 240 in 1989 to number 89 in 1990, at which time Slater became a professional surfer at just eighteen years old. As an amateur he had won money, but as a minor the bulk of Slater's competitive winnings from all of his early competitions was placed in a trust fund.

Becoming a professional surfer had immediate financial benefits for Slater. Now, not only could he win—and keep—the money, but his performance in competitions and his innovative, aggressive style also led to corporate sponsorship of Quiksilver. At the age of eighteen, Slater signed a three-and-a-half-year contract to endorse the company's products. For this, Slater would be paid $1 million. Slater's first expenditure was to pay off the remainder of his mother's home mortgage. She had supported and believed in his ability throughout his childhood, and now he was in a position to repay the favor.

Meanwhile, although travel to various competitions had caused him to miss school, Slater worked toward high school graduation. In

1991, Slater graduated high school with a 4.0 grade point average. That same year, he increased his world surfing rank by more than half, coming in at number forty-three among active surfers. The cut-off for the World Championship Tour was forty-four, so he would be allowed to compete on the tour in 1992. He was also named one of *People* magazine's fifty most beautiful people for 1991. Now Slater was not only popular among surfers, but he also gained a celebrity following thanks to his appearance in the magazine.

In what would prove to be his best year yet, 1992 brought Slater his first World Cup victory, as well as victories at the Marui Masters and Pro Landes contests. His greatest victory, however, came that same year at the Pro Junior tournament in New South Wales, Australia, since he was the first American to ever win that event. Also, since the grand total points earned in all his competitions that year topped the totals of all world competitors, Slater was named the Association of Surfing Professionals (ASP) world champion for 1992. He was just twenty years old.

Jimmy Slade

As if the feat of becoming world champion were not enough, during the same year Slater received a different opportunity through his agent. He appeared as Jimmy Slade, a buff, tanned surf bum on the hit television series *Baywatch*. In addition, it was on the set of the series that he met Pamela Anderson, who played the part of a lifeguard on the show. The two began a high-profile Hollywood relationship, constantly hounded by tabloid media and adoring fans. During their on-and-off relationship, the two traveled to Slater's childhood home of Cocoa Beach, as well as to Hawaii and Fiji.

Slater gained visibility among the nonsurfing public through his role on *Baywatch*, but he also received much criticism from his fellow surfers. They felt that his character simply promoted the negative stereotypes that had haunted the sport for decades. Slater explains how he responded to the criticism: "I begged to get off the show. The motivation was 30 percent me just wanting to be a serious athlete and 70 percent surfers saying, 'Slater made a mockery of surfing, there's no forgiveness.' But I used that grudge against those guys to drive myself harder, and I won my first world title that year." [29]

Slater continued with *Baywatch* for the 1993 season before quitting to surf full time. In 1994, however, Slater was in front of the camera once again, with a small role in *The Endless Summer II*. The film, with its stylish depiction of surf culture, became an instant classic among surf aficionados throughout the world. Slater also played

Slater smacks the lip of a wave in Tahiti. Slater's aggressive surfing style won him six world champion titles.

a much larger role in the video, *Kelly Slater in Black and White.* The tape, which consists of Slater surfing famous breaks and popular competitions around the world, became the highest-selling surf video of all time.

Record-Breaking Wins for the World's Greatest Surfer

Meanwhile, Slater returned to the ranks of surfing's elite. While he tied for fifth place in the ASP world championship in 1993, Slater would come back to win the title of world champion for the next five consecutive years, 1994–1998. This feat set a world record for any surfer in history, as did winning six times overall. Of this period, Slater would later cite 1996, when he won half of the fourteen events he entered, as his best year. His wins included Australia's Coke Surf Classic, the U.S. Open, and France's Rip Curl competition.

Kelly Slater also became a father in 1996. A baby girl, Taylor, was born on June 4 to a woman whom Slater dated. Taylor's mother, a former model, had met Slater when he was still in high school. Although Slater did not share in custody of the child, he would continue to see Taylor on a regular basis, often taking her on vacations to various coastal resorts.

After earning his sixth world championship in 1998, Slater decided to take a break from surfing. He went into what he called a semiretirement, entering only a handful of competitions as the mood struck him. At the age of twenty-six, Slater had enough money from his sponsorship and winnings to last a lifetime, and he had experienced more fame than any other surfer in the history of the sport. He felt that he had focused so much of his energy on surfing over the past twenty-one years that he needed to diversify and experience other aspects of life. At the time he explained his motivation for setting surfing aside: "Now that I've succeeded at every goal I ever set, I'm basically taking this year off to look for a new fuel source. I was winning on anger, but I used all the angry energy up. I used to be able to fire up for anyone who'd beaten me in a heat, anyone who said anything negative in a magazine. I tried not just to win heats, but to dominate them, smother the other guys, kill them." [30] Slater set aside his competitive urges in order to relax and enjoy the beauty of surfing.

A Break from the Pressures of Competition

Over the years, faced with an abundance of free time on shore waiting for good waves to break, Slater kept himself occupied by learning to play guitar. His interest in guitar soon evolved into playing in a band he had begun with two other pro surfers, Rob Machado and Peter King, appropriately called The Surfers. The trio released their first album, *Songs from the Pipe*, in 1998. The band also played a benefit on the island of Oahu to increase awareness of overcrowding in the already-packed Honolulu area.

Slater also took advantage of his time off to brush up on his golf, a game which he felt had something in common with surfing in that both sports required absolute concentration. Slater discovered that by watching the top pros, he could use his imagination to visualize ways of improving his golf swing, just as he could imagine himself catching a wave:

> Watching Tiger and Ernie Els really improved my swing, because I can watch them and know how it would feel to hit it that way, and then try to reproduce it. Just like I can watch

Slater carries his big-wave board across the beach of Oahu's Waimea Bay before a competition. Fellow surfers still dreaded drawing a heat against Slater during his semiretirement.

a wave and surf it in my mind, know precisely how it feels. I can even feel the little foot movements I would do to stall or get more speed. It would take a whole paragraph to describe just one move, but I don't even think about it.[31]

Yet, even during retirement, Slater thought about surfing incessantly. For this reason, Slater elected not to abandon competition altogether. He entered and won the Pipe Master's event at Pipeline, Hawaii, for the fifth year in a row in 1999; he also spent time surfing accompanied by his friend Eddie Vedder, of the band Pearl Jam, in the Tasman Sea off the coast of Australia.

Slater describes surfing as a relationship similar to a close friendship that requires nurturing:

I notice that when I don't surf very much, when I go back out there, things just aren't gonna go my way. Obviously, part of that is due to the physical aspect of the sport, but I also sort of take it like the ocean's a friend of mine, and you gotta respect it like a friend. You know, if you don't call your friend for a month, they're gonna be pissed off. They'll be like, "I thought you cared about me." To me it's sort of the same thing with surfing.[32]

Surf Exploration in the Indian Ocean

In June 2001, Kelly Slater hopped aboard a boat called the *Indies Trader* for a portion of the Quiksilver Crossing, an expedition that combined surfing with scientific study. The boat had been traveling the South Pacific since March 1999, its passengers exploring new surf spots, examining coral reefs for the United Nations Reef Check program, and studying indigenous cultures. For his part in the tour, Slater assembled a group of seven other elite surfers to explore undiscovered surf breaks in the northern islands of the Indian Ocean. Slater explains the objective of the trip was "to explore new regions and to avoid populated surfing areas as much as possible. On this trip we are looking for new waves in a rarely visited region of the Indian Ocean." [33] To visually document the trip, three cinematographers with a variety of cameras and two still photographers came along. Slater's two-week stint on the boat, called *Outside the Boundaries,* was broadcast over the Internet.

Video Slater

Upon returning from his Indian Ocean journey, Slater focused much of his time on a new venture, creating and marketing the video game *Kelly Slater: Pro Surfer.* In the game, he and a group of surfing friends, including Kalani Robb, Tom Curren, and Rob Machado, travel the world to thirteen of the best surfing destinations. Using a joystick, the game player can manipulate a selected surfer through a series of stunts and tricks on the virtual waves of the television screen. To promote the game, these surfers produced a film documenting a week they spent living and surfing together on the North Shore of Oahu. The film was aired in the summer of 2002 on ESPN.

Slater's expedition to the Indian Ocean and the work on the video game rekindled his appetite for surfing full time, causing him to enter the Quiksilver In Memory of Eddie Aikau Contest at Oahu's Waimea Bay in January 2002. Slater quickly showed not only that his competitive spirit was still there, but that he was still the best. At the end of the competition, Slater was ranked second. When he rechecked the judge's math, however, he found that he had actually won, and he forced the judges to correct their mistake. Yearning for the chance to prove himself king once more, Slater decided to end his three-year retirement to compete in the 2002 world tour.

To Surf or Not to Surf?

A major part of winning the world title, Slater knew, lay in knowing the strengths and weaknesses of his opponents. Many of the same surfers were competing still, but there were new faces among the professionals, so Slater began training rigorously and studying the competition. Thanks to his preparation, even though he had been off the tour for some while, Slater felt confident in his chances of a successful comeback.

The first world contest of the year, Australia's Quiksilver Pro, led fans to believe that Slater might very well win a seventh world title, but unforseen circumstances on the homefront forced him to defer his comeback. Just as the 2002 tour was about to get underway, Slater's father, Stephen, was diagnosed with terminal cancer. The news of his father's illness came as a shock and Slater was unable to focus on training or competition.

In early spring of 2002, Steve Slater passed away. Slater explains his feelings at the news of his father's death.

> Obviously it's a really sad thing, but I don't feel sad when I think about him. . . . I start laughing and remember how funny he was and how happy and positive he was all the time. Even when he was ill, he was positive about life. . . . He didn't feel like he wasted any time not enjoying it. . . . When he found out he had cancer, his life changed drastically. Our family got closer together, and there was a lot of good that came out of that.[34]

He failed to make his much-anticipated return to full-time surfing, but the fact that he had spent time with his father did help to bring some closure to Slater's grief.

Reflections of a Retired Thirty-Year-Old Millionaire

Even though 2002 did not turn out to be the year Kelly Slater made his comeback, he still views his life as fulfilling. With six world titles under his belt, numerous appearances in film and television, multiple corporate sponsors, and a video game with his name on it, Slater can afford to take it easy. Yet, when he reflects on what truly makes him happy he rejects the idea that his happiness depends on wealth, instead explaining that "I think what's wrong with America is that we don't really know what happiness is. We have society that is telling us things. . . . From the time we're born we're influenced to believe that money is the root of all happiness. And it's not. Happiness is being comfortable with yourself." [35]

CHAPTER 4

Lynn Hill: A Free Climbing Revolutionary

Resting 2,500 feet above sea level on a rock ledge, Lynn Hill contemplated the next sequence of moves. Five hundred feet of intensely strenuous climbing lay between her and the summit of Yosemite's El Capitan, one of the world's tallest granite monoliths. Though it had been climbed countless times since the first ascent in 1958, Hill was preparing to climb a long blank section of glassy granite, with virtually no holds for hands or feet. She had been climbing with little rest since ten o'clock at night.

Now, nineteen-and-a-half hours later, she was watching the sun begin to fade over the western hills. She had less than five hours left to meet her goal of completing one of North America's tallest and hardest climbs in a single day. She explains the climb's importance:

> This ascent was symbolic of the kind of values that give meaning and richness to my climbing experience. Throughout my life, one of the underlying qualities that has inspired me to pursue my vision of what is possible has to do with trusting in what I truly love and believe in. Cultivating such feelings of passion and conviction is what has enabled me to tap the source of my being and access the immense power of the human spirit.[36]

All of the events of Hill's life served as preparation for this very moment. Her childhood training as a gymnast, her early climbing experience, her competitive sport climbing career, and her extensive knowledge of the route combined to form this instant in which she must perform her most challenging climb.

Growing Up Independent

Lynn Hill entered the world in Detroit, Michigan, on January 3, 1961, the fifth of seven children born to parents James and Suzanne Hill. The Hill family moved to Columbus, Ohio, shortly after Lynn's birth, where her father pursued a doctorate in flight mechanics. With seven children, Suzanne Hill stayed busy with the full-time job of raising such a large family. Later, once the children were grown, she worked as a dental hygienist. After receiving his degree, James Hill took a job as an aerospace engineer with North American Rockwell. This position prompted the family's move to Fullerton, California.

When Lynn was a child, Fullerton, a suburb of Los Angeles, was an ideal place to grow up. The kids rode their bikes everywhere, appreciating the freedom of the outdoors. Lynn's parents supported this love of nature by vacationing often throughout California's vast array of lakes, mountains, and parks. The Hill family consisted of four boys and three girls, each separated in age by roughly one year. In the rough and tumble of such a large family, young Lynn learned to fend for herself and evolved into a self-proclaimed tomboy, engaging in such activities as playing with snakes and climbing telephone poles.

Competing at an Early Age

Hill took an interest in competitive sports at an early age. Her first experience in competition came at the age of seven when she entered a swim meet. She finished first, but was disqualified because she neglected to actually touch the wall at the finish. Lynn learned a vital lesson that day: be more concerned with the fine points of performance than with winning.

The sport, however, for which Lynn showed an early talent was gymnastics, and by the age of ten, she was competing throughout Southern California. The challenge of manipulating her body to overcome the forces of gravity attracted Hill to the sport. Through gymnastics, Hill learned to break a routine into parts or "chunks." This process allowed her to understand complex moves in simpler form and then combine them to create a sense of full, fluid motion. In preparing for competitions, Hill would train her body to follow whatever gymnastic sequences her mind produced.

In 1973, however, at the age of twelve Hill gave up competitive gymnastics altogether. She did so because she found herself more interested in the actual physical nature of movement than the contests themselves. Hill wanted to expand her ability to perform and link together complex, gravity-defying moves without the hindrance of worrying about competitions and the opinions of judges. She would soon get just such a chance on the rock walls and cliffs of Southern California.

First Steps in the Vertical World

Hill found that her gymnastic training and balance made her a natural at climbing rocks. In 1975, family friend Chuck Bludworth drove Hill and some of her siblings to Big Rock, a small climbing area in Southern California. Hill was immediately hooked on rock climbing. She explains the lure the sport offered her, saying, "The fact that you're alone out there, even if you're climbing with some-body, when you're actually on the rock it's you and the rock. . . . The reasons you succeeded or the reasons you fell are your own, and you can learn from them."[37] Through rock climbing, Hill learned to set her own goals and standards, instead of following those established by a panel of judges.

Chuck Bludworth became one of Hill's main inspirations and early supporters. Bludworth did not let his ego and fear of being outdone by a young girl get in the way of teaching her everything he knew. Instead, Bludworth helped Lynn cultivate her own natural ability on the rock. Natural ability was something that Hill had in abundance. Within months of her first climbing experience, Hill was climbing routes that some people aspire for years to complete.

California Cragging: Joshua Tree and Yosemite

Lynn Hill's natural prowess soon attracted the attention of a group of vagabond climbers who frequented the cliffs located in Joshua Tree National Monument. Her ability to perform incredibly hard

The craggy rock formations of Joshua Tree National Monument offer vertical challenges for capable climbers. Lynn Hill developed an interest in climbing at Joshua Tree.

climbs drew admirers from this ragged bunch who called themselves "Stonemasters," and they soon accepted her into their fold. The Stonemasters were elite climbers who made a point of establishing challenging climbing routes that required the most sophisticated moves.

Joshua Tree offered its share of challenges, but hearing about the abundance of climbing in Yosemite National Park, Hill spent the summer of 1978 there. At Yosemite, she met more climbers who were pushing the vertical limits of the day. Some held jobs or attended school, but others were full-time climbers who funded their unpaid career by waiting tables, collecting aluminum cans, or simply panhandling from tourists. Some other members of the Stonemasters also were denizens of Yosemite. Among the many familiar faces from her Joshua Tree days was John Long. Shortly after her arrival in Yosemite, Hill began dating Long, who introduced her to the life of a climbing bum.

Free Climbing the Big Walls of Yosemite

Long also introduced Hill to a form of the sport that was gaining popularity, free climbing. Like participants in the more established aid climbing, free climbers place either removable gear or permanent metal hooks called pitons or bolts securely in the rock face. How climbers use the equipment distinguishes free climbers from aid climbers. Aid climbers use their gear to pull themselves up hard sections of a route in a ladderlike fashion, whereas free climbers rely on the ropes they attach to the gear only to protect them in the event of a fall. While those who pioneered the sport of climbing sought to reach the top of a rock wall by whatever means necessary, free climbers move up attached to the cliff by a rope, but touching only naturally formed rock with their hands and feet. Climbers break routes up into sections called pitches; at the end of a pitch a climber can rest and consider the moves to come.

Hill became almost a fixture on the big walls of Yosemite, where she first honed her climbing skills. She first climbed the Nose on El Capitan in the summer of 1979 with two of her friends, Mari Gingery and Dean Fidelman. Using a mixture of aid and free climbing tactics, they spent three nights on the wall. This first exposure to such an immense climb inspired Hill to push her limits in the realm of free climbing. She recalls her experience. "Frazzled certainly described our condition as we each popped over the rim of El Cap. We were hungry, thirsty, and bone tired . . . I peered over the rim . . . It was a view I felt comfortable with." [38]

The Nose was Hill's introduction to big wall climbing, and it whetted her appetite for more. She and Mari Gingery teamed up again to climb the Shield, a more difficult route on El Cap. After six days and twenty-nine pitches, they completed the ascent—the first all-female team to do so.

Pushing the Grade

After gaining vital experience on the big walls of Yosemite, Hill decided to devote her climbing efforts to extremely hard climbs on smaller cliffs. Free climbing these routes had natural attraction to a self-driven athlete like Hill, since they required her to perform at the top of her ability. In the early 1980s, Hill traveled with John Long around the United States, settling briefly in various towns near popular climbing areas. One particularly memorable climb she made was the first free ascent of a route known as Ophir Broke in Telluride, Colorado. She explains the lesson she learned that day. "No matter what our physical differences, with the right combination of vision, desire, and effort, just about any climb was possible. Short or tall, man or woman, the rock is an objective medium that is equally open for interpretation by all." [39]

Hill and Long shared many experiences together during their relationship, but eventually they came to understand that their lives were headed in different directions. Long was interested in seeking fame in Hollywood as a filmmaker and writer, while Hill wanted to attend college and earn a degree in biology. Tired of the traveling and the hand-to-mouth existence of a climbing bum, Hill moved to New Paltz, New York, where she enrolled at the local branch of the State University of New York. During this time she continued to push her limits while climbing on the steep cliffs of the nearby Shawangunk Mountains. Shortly after her arrival in New Paltz, Hill began dating Russ Raffa, a local climber who showed her the best routes in the area. In 1986 the two toured Europe together to train and climb.

Competitive Climbing

The trip to Europe was Hill's introduction to competitive climbing. She was invited to compete in the Sport Roccio climbing competition in Arco, Italy. Rather than merely climbing fast, she wanted to climb precisely, without falling. As a result, although Hill was the only woman in the competition to complete the final route, she still placed second because the judges based their decision more on speed than on actual completion of the route. This contest and those that followed, much like her early gymnastics meets, were frustrating for Hill, but they also reignited her competitive nature. During this time, Hill's reason for climbing shifted from recreation and self-fulfillment to a more competitive motivation.

Lynn Hill rests on a perch during an ascent at the Shawangunk Mountains in New York. Hill's childhood training as a gymnast gave her the strength and balance to climb the world's toughest cliffs.

Even though the judges' standards and requirements angered Hill, she continued to climb competitively throughout Europe and the United States for the next three years. Hill found success by combining her technical knowledge of climbing with her gymnastic ability to focus on the immediate task and break complex routines into smaller parts. Hill won the majority of the competitions she entered and used the prize money from these victories to support her travels, in the process becoming a professional climber.

In the midst of this travel and competition, Lynn Hill and Russ Raffa were married in October of 1988. The two maintained a home in New York, while Hill traveled the United States and Europe as a professional climber. Russ worked as a product representative for the outdoor industry, so he traveled a great deal as well. The two seldom spent time together due to their equally demanding work schedules.

Moving from place to place while attempting to stay in top physical form took its toll on Hill. This aspect of competition weighed on her and detracted from the reasons she loved climbing in the first place. The constant time away from her home and husband was hard on the marriage as well. Despite these difficulties, Hill became the number one woman climber in sport competition by the year 1989. She was scheduled to compete in climbing's first ever World Cup competition when disaster struck.

Fall from Grace

While climbing the route Buffet Froid in Buoux, France, Hill experienced every climber's nightmare. She completed the climb with relative ease, but as she sat back to lower off the cliff, she realized too late that the rope was not tied into her harness. The rope is the climber's link to safety. To do any good, the rope must be securely fastened to the climber's waist harness. In a split second, the unknotted rope slid through her harness and she fell over seventy feet to the ground below.

Hill was lucky. She suffered relatively minor injuries, such as a dislocated arm, cuts to her chest, and black eyes. Of greater importance regarding her future as a professional athlete, the accident left her questioning whether she would ever climb competitively again. Hill knew, however, that if she did not return to climbing as soon as her physical condition would allow, that she might never return to the sport. True to her determined spirit, she resumed training as soon as her bandages were off.

Three months after her fall, Hill began competing once again, but found that, much like her early swimming experience, she was focusing more on winning than climbing to the best of her ability. The pressures of traveling and competing continued to affect Hill, and although she continued climbing competitively she also refocused attention on free climbing hard routes in the natural outdoor environment.

During this time, Lynn and Russ were experiencing marital problems. All of the travel and time apart weighed heavily on the relationship; as a consequence, much of the time they did spend together was taken up with discussion about their marriage. Their busy lives were leading in two different directions, and by the spring of 1991, they mutually decided to divorce.

The hectic schedule and hard training that had contributed to the break up of her marriage left Hill questioning what she was doing, and in 1992 she decided to quit competing professionally. Out of the thirty-eight competitions she had entered, she won twenty-six. Yet, while winning brought her fame and cash prizes, competition did not challenge her or bring her as much joy as free climbing outdoors did. Hill came to understand that she could use her natural climbing ability for a more meaningful purpose than simply winning competitions.

Free Climbing the Nose

Still in top form from six years of competitive climbing, Hill focused her efforts on a personal objective: climbing a route that involved a high level of technical difficulty on the big wall terrain she loved the most. She describes her decision, saying, "In the aftermath of my competition career what I wanted most of all was the freedom to pursue rock climbing again in the beautiful natural environment. One challenge that had long been lingering in the back of my mind came to surface: to free climb 'the Nose.' "[40]

Many climbers had tried to take on Yosemite's most famous route to the top of El Capitan, but none managed to complete all thirty-three pitches without using some man-made device to gain ground. Two sections of the route, the Great Roof and the Changing Corners, had never been free climbed before. In the fall of 1993, Hill made her first attempt at free climbing the Nose in the company of British climber Simon Nadin. Although the duo made it past the Great Roof, they failed to get past the Changing Corners section. The main problem was ten feet of blank rock that seemed impassable.

Hill would not accept defeat that easily. Several weeks later she returned with a new partner, Brooke Sandahl. The two climbers, in order to get a different perspective on the problem, used ropes to rappel from the top of El Capitan to the Changing Corners pitch.

El Capitan in Yosemite is one of the greatest climbing challenges in the United States. After making several aided ascents up El Capitan, Hill focused on free climbing the giant granite monolith.

Once there, they spent three days determining the sequence of moves necessary to overcome this obstacle. With boosted confidence, the pair returned several days later to begin their all-free ascent of the Nose. The days of training paid off as Hill strongly climbed through the sequence that had given her so much trouble before. She recalls the moment of success. "When I reached the belay, I felt a tingle of disbelief run through me. Though we had several pitches to go, none were as hard as this one."[41] With newfound energy, Hill finished the rest of the route and camped on top of El Capitan. She had successfully completed an all-free ascent of the classic Nose route.

Pushing the Limits Further

Even as she basked in her accomplishment, Hill already had bigger plans. Although she had climbed the entire route free, she now set her sights on completing the entire climb in a single day. Just staying awake for twenty-four hours would be hard, but attempting to climb three thousand feet of incredibly technical rock in that time period would be extremely difficult. Hill trained for endurance and power, both of which she would need in abundance to fulfill her new goal.

Hill chose longtime friend Steve Sutton as her partner. On September 19, 1994, at 10:00 in the evening, they started climbing the lower pitches by the light of the full moon and arrived at the Great Roof pitch some ten hours later. After a short nap under the roof, Hill tackled this section, which had so challenged her in the past. Calm and focused from her rest, she climbed with all of her strength and finesse. Just before 10:30 A.M., Hill successfully stood at the belay above the Great Roof with almost twelve hours left to meet her goal. The pair continued to climb through the heat of the day until they reached the Changing Corners pitch. There they rested until the sun was no longer shining directly on the rock, about 5:30 in the afternoon.

Shortly into her first motions on the pitch, Hill realized she had made a crucial mistake. Although the route was in the shade by this time, it was still too hot for making the delicate moves required to negotiate the almost featureless rock face. She fell onto the rope, frustrated at her first mistake of the day. After several more failed attempts, she began to wonder if she could actually finish the route, because she had only four hours left. Hill describes her final attempt at the pitch. "This time I knew that it was critical to remain patient and not rush into the next crucial 'Houdini' move . . . the sequences flowed together . . . I was extremely happy to finally make it on my last try. Free climbing this pitch in such a fatigued state had required a greater effort than any climb I had done before."[42]

Hill continued to climb upward as the light faded, and ended up at the last pitch in the dark. With all the strength she could muster, she contorted her body to fit the sequence of moves by the light of a headlamp. Hill reached the summit, fully exhausted after twenty-three hours of effort. She recalls, "My mind swirled in an other-worldly state, yet I felt an underlying sense of peace and serenity. In my dreamlike trance, I knew it was not possible to comprehend all that I had just experienced on this journey. In fact, it has taken me years to fully digest what took place that day."[43]

Lynn Hill was not only the first person to free climb the Nose, but now she had accomplished that incredible feat in under a day.

Hill scales the underside of a hanging cliff face. Despite suffering a serious fall in 1989, Hill continues to push herself to conquer the world's most difficult climbs.

She felt that the climb's significance was more than just a personal triumph.

> I think that "The Nose" climb actually was a statement for me about people doing what they're capable of, no matter what the perceived difficulties are. If you're small, if you're tall, whatever your body type or sex, it doesn't really matter. If you want to do a climb and you've worked at it, it's not unreasonable. . . . Why be limited by what other people say?[44]

Hill's Reflections on Her Career

With more than twenty-five years of climbing experience, Hill is an incredibly versatile climber. Her early days of aid and free climbing in California and New York taught her technical lessons, and climbing competitively honed her style and grace. Hill was able to combine these skills in order to accomplish the phenomenal feat of climbing the Nose in one day. She describes the meaning of that accomplishment for her, saying, "The magnificent beauty and historic significance of the line—as well as my own efforts to free it, and later free it in a day—made this ascent the most meaningful achievement of my climbing career."[45]

Lynn Hill continues to be active in the climbing scene. She describes her current goals:

> I would like to continue my journeys on the rock in beautiful places around the world. What I love most about climbing is the beauty and diversity of the environment and the different rock types, climbing styles, and the people with whom I share these experiences. No matter how things evolve in the future, one element that seems to remain constant is my desire to continue climbing, exploring new heights.[46]

Her exploits have taken her to Kyrgyzstan, Morocco, Vietnam, Thailand, Scotland, Japan, Australia, South America, Madagascar, and all over Europe. When she is not traveling the globe, she lives in Boulder, Colorado, a town that is renowned for its abundance of nearby climbing opportunities.

CHAPTER 5

Ned Overend: The Father of Mountain Bike Racing

Known as the father of mountain bike racing, Ned Overend has spent his career learning to balance, both on his bicycle and in his personal life. A competitive athlete since his early teens, Overend exemplifies the discipline and persistence necessary to become both a national and a world mountain bike champion multiple times. What makes Overend's accomplishments even more astounding is that he has managed to compete and win at endurance sports into his late forties, dominating competitors who are half his age.

A Youthful World Traveler

Ned Overend was born far from his current home in the Colorado mountains. His father, Edmund Overend, worked in the U.S. State Department's Aid to Foreign Countries Program. One of six children, Ned was born in Tapei, Taiwan, on August 20, 1955. He lived in both Iran and Ethiopia in the late 1950s and much of the 1960s. Ned's mother, Helen, was a homemaker during this time, patiently enduring the need to relocate the family every few years as a result of her husband's diplomatic post.

Also as a result of his father's job, Ned did not live in the United States until he was a teenager. Eventually, however, the family settled in Marin County, California, north of San Francisco. Not long after, in 1971, Edmund Overend died of a heart attack. Helen was left to look after the family, relying on her husband's pension and later working at a bank to make ends meet.

As a high school freshman, Ned ran cross-country and rode motorcross. Although both sports have a loose team aspect, Ned took to the solitude and self-motivation involved with running and riding the trails. Ned was influenced by his high school cross-country coach, Doug Basham, whom he described as "a strong runner who did several workouts with the team. He emphasized quality training, while being careful to avoid over-training and injury. He would also have us do a variety of workouts to keep it fresh." [47]

Early Training and Altitude Experience

Overend continued running throughout his high school years and into college. He ran both track and cross-country at both the College of Marin and the College of the Redwoods. Running was something at which Overend excelled, and he was selected for the California Junior College All-State Cross-Country Team in 1976.

Despite his ability as a distance runner, the race that changed Overend's life was one he entered on a whim in 1980. That year he decided to register for the Hawaiian Ironman Triathlon, a competition that included bike riding and swimming in addition to running. Winners were determined by the fastest total time of all three events. Relatively inexperienced at swimming and cycling, Overend relied on his ability as a runner to pull him through the race, and although he had little training, he placed twenty-fourth out of more than a hundred competitors.

Making Big Decisions for the Future

That very same year, Overend met the woman who would one day be his wife. Pam, a native of San Diego who was working as a nurse and Ned, who had a job as a car mechanic, met at a disco. The two had a brief courtship in California, and decided to make a life together. They settled not in California but in the more mountainous terrain of Durango, Colorado, an ideal location in which Overend could continue to pursue his avocation as a long-distance runner. Overend got a job as a mechanic for a shop called Precision Imports, while Pam found work in the community's hospital. The two were married the following year, in 1981.

The mountains of Colorado, though much higher than those Overend was used to in California and Hawaii, did not stop him from excelling at his sport. He placed second in the Pike's Peak Marathon in 1981 and 1982. He also set records for two other famous races in Colorado, the Kendall Mountain Run and the Estes Park Triathlon. Estes was particularly challenging, since the race includes an eighty-mile bike ride through Rocky Mountain National Park, twenty-six miles of running, and a mile of lap swimming—all at an elevation greater than 8,000 feet.

The more difficult the course, the greater the climb, and the higher the altitude, the better Overend seemed to perform, earning him the nickname "The Lung." Encouraged by his success in triathlons, Ned also began entering road bike races in 1982. He took to the sport immediately, and began winning both beginner and advanced categories in his first year of competition. Noticing his natural ability as a racer, Raleigh Bicycles offered Overend a spot on their team for the 1983 Coors Classic, the most prestigious road race in the United States at the time. Overend describes his excitement at competing in the event: "All the best teams in the world were there, the Italians,

A pack of riders climbs a steep pass. After riding road bikes during a triathlon, Ned Overend was led down a twenty-year career path in competitive mountain bike racing.

the French, and the East Germans who won. It was brutal, and I didn't do real well, but it was a real slice of bike racing for a guy who had only started riding a year earlier." [48]

Ned Overend switched jobs in 1983 to one that was closely related to his interest in bike racing: a mechanic's position at a bike shop, the Outdoorsman. Now his weeks were filled learning the inner workings of bicycles, and his weekends consisted of entering and winning various bike races around the United States. Overend quickly proved himself. In his second year of racing bicycles professionally, he was named Colorado's best overall rider in 1983.

Ned Discovers the Mountain Bike

Around this time Overend discovered the mountain bike, a relatively new type of bicycle designed for riding on trails in addition to roads.

Overend edges out a competitor during an off-road race. The individuality of mountain bike racing drew Overend to the sport.

Overend borrowed a cheap Schwinn mountain bike from The Out-doorsman and took it along on vacation in California. There, Overend entered and won several of the Pacific Suntour Series races. His performance in California prompted Schwinn to sponsor him for the finals a few weeks later. The company's support paid off when Overend won the race.

Overend believes the individuality involved in competitive mountain biking attracted him, explaining "Mountain bike racing is more of an individual sport. In road racing, you have to worry about teamwork and tactics. In mountain biking, you're on your own. The strongest and fittest rider usually wins." [49] Another factor that attracted Overend to mountain bike racing was that it did not require as much travel and time away from home as road racing did. This decision was important to Overend and Pam, who gave birth to their daughter Alison that year.

Sponsorship and Success

At this point, Overend began riding the trails full time, although he entered a dozen or more road races each year because he felt road riding was good training for mountain biking. With Schwinn as his sponsor, he was able to upgrade to a lighter bike with more durable components and receive funding for travel and races.

At the dawning of this new sport, Overend became the poster child for mountain bike racing and one of the sport's first sponsored athletes. Under the direction of fellow mountain biker Glen Odell, several cyclists formed the National Off-Road Bicycle Association (NORBA). The group acted as a governing body for U.S. mountain biking and began staging races across the country that year. Overend placed second in the NORBA National Championships in 1984 and fifth in 1985. The national winner for both years, Joe Murray, had lost to Overend in California's Suntour Series a year earlier, so Overend knew he stood a strong chance of winning this prestigious trophy.

Overend fulfilled his goal by winning the NORBA National Championship for both 1986 and 1987. As the sport boomed in the United States, the rest of the world began to take notice of mountain biking. New companies began to emerge with more performance-oriented bikes, and Schwinn's quality and innovation were eventually surpassed by some of these newcomers. In 1987 Overend switched sponsorship to one of these newer companies called Specialized. Overend chose the company because ". . . they were dedicated to racing, and committed to developing the best products in the world . . . they never pressured me to perform, they just supported me with good equipment, mechanics and designers." [50]

That same year, NORBA staged a world championship for hill climbing and cross-country riding, both of which Overend won. By inviting competitors from around the world, the sport gained more global appeal, thereby further ensuring its continued popularity. Not only was he the best in the nation, but Overend was the world's greatest mountain biker in 1987.

While he placed second in the nation for 1988, Overend's performance in the NORBA World Championships that year went into the record books as one of the greatest comebacks in the sport. Overend immediately ran into trouble in the first of five laps, when his rear tire went flat. Having to replace the tube on the trailside cost him four minutes of precious time. Now the tenacity for which Overend was already becoming famous came into play. On the last lap, he passed the leader, John Tomac, to secure the victory. Gritty performances such as that became Overend's signature; just when competitors thought they had him beat, he would pass them, more than likely in the most grueling uphill section of the course, to steal the win. Such come-from-behind wins earned him another nickname, "Deadly Nedly." In 1989, Overend regained his national title, and placed fourth in the world championships.

World Mountain Biking and The Hall of Fame

With the steady growth of mountain biking, the world's governing body of all bicycling, the Union Cycliste Internationale, sanctioned their first world mountain biking championship in 1990. While NORBA had sponsored such an event for the past two years, having this highly prestigious, established organization recognize and support mountain biking was a huge step for the evolution of the sport. This first world championship was held on Overend's home turf in Durango. Overend won the race, thus claiming the title of world champion for the third time. He won the NORBA national title once again in 1990, and became the first inductee into the Mountain Biking Hall of Fame. Mountain biking was now an officially recognized sport, and Overend, at the age of thirty-five, was the strongest athlete in his field.

For the next two years, Overend held onto his NORBA national title, beating opponents half his age with hard work and confidence. At the age of thirty-seven, most athletes, especially those with a wife and family, either begin coaching or retire to take up less physically demanding pursuits. While he was always ready to lend advice and help other cyclists, Overend refused to give up competition, despite the fact that he and Pam now had a second child, a boy named Rhyler.

Overend rides up a rock during training. Remaining in peak physical condition over the years earned Overend the nickname "The Lung."

The Lung Retires

Ned Overend continued to race mountain bikes professionally for the next five years, winning competitions in the United States and abroad. In 1996, at forty-one years of age, Overend officially retired from full-time bike racing because he wanted to spend more time with his family. He continued to race in several events, but no longer followed the sport full time.

Overend looked back on his time as a professional racer with a combination of joy and regret. Although his life had been easy in the sense of only having to focus on winning races, it had also been a stressful existence. In an interview with Zapata Espinoza, Overend explains:

> There's a feeling that you can only get from racing and finishing—the feeling of pushing yourself to the absolute limit beyond what you're capable of. . . . It's about achieving the

ultimate physical accomplishment. . . . The hardest part about being a pro racer is that . . . the pressure to perform is always there, no matter what you're doing. Racing has been the most intense part of my life.[51]

While mountain bike racing had been the major focus of Overend's sports career from 1984–1996, he looked forward to branching out and participating in other activities in his semiretirement.

The Secret to Ned's Success

Rather than looking at his family and his job commitments as a distraction from his training and race performance, Overend saw his busy schedule as the main reason for his success and longevity in a sport normally dominated by competitors half his age. An avid reader of training and coaching manuals, he understood the importance of balance in a workout.

For Overend, taking time off from training to spend time with his family and participate in other interests away from cycling was of great importance. Overend's commitment to his family and the desire to push himself in a wide array of training activities made him a well-balanced athlete. In a sport in which many competitors often overtrain and burn out both mentally and physically, he maintained a strong competitive edge while managing to enjoy himself along the way.

A Race Just for Overend

Overend, however, was not about to put himself out to pasture even though he had retired from the professional mountain bike circuit. He was intrigued by a chance to combine his beloved trail and mountain biking with the opportunity to experience the challenges of triathlons and road races. The Nissan XTERRA Championships, which began the same year that Overend retired from mountain biking, offered just such an opportunity.

The entire concept of the XTERRA competition fit with Overend's cross-training philosophy. Instead of just focusing on one sport, the contest called for well-rounded athletes who could excel at a multitude of sports. Overend describes the XTERRA event and his choice to compete in it, saying,

I still needed something to train and stay in shape for, and that's when the XTERRA thing was starting. . . . The whole event is similar to a mountain bike race in that it's like a time trial—you're going hard the whole time for about two and a half hours. . . . A lot of it is just getting your body used to the different activities with no time to adjust in between.[52]

In his first two years of the competition, Overend placed in the top three, but he came back to win both the 1998 and 1999 XTERRA World Championships in Maui, Hawaii. He continued to race the event in 2000 and 2001, placing in the top five both years.

With only approximately six XTERRA events each year, Overend managed to enter other events as well, such as the 2001 U.S.A. Triathlon Winter National Championships in Winter Park, Colorado.

Overend test rides a Specialized mountain bike. Overend's many victories have earned him a place in the U.S. Bicycling Hall of Fame.

The blustery conditions added a twist to the ten-kilometer run and the twenty-kilometer mountain bike course, as the trails were covered in packed snow with six inches of fresh snow accumulating during the race itself. The third stage of the contest involved cross-country skiing for ten kilometers through the resort's wooded trail system. Overend placed first in the race, proving that even at the age of forty-five, he was a major force to contend with.

Ned Refuses to Act His Age

Overend attributed his longevity in high-endurance competition to his sensible workout routine and his multi-sport and life balance. Although it took him longer to recover from hard training days and grueling competitions, he listened to his body and understood that his muscles rebuild themselves during the rest period that follows a workout, not during the workout itself. He also did not allow himself to get caught up in winning or losing, but focused on doing his best and enjoying himself.

While he already held the title of first inductee to the Mountain Bike Hall of Fame in 1990, Overend received another high honor in May 2001 when he was inducted into the U.S. Bicycling Hall of Fame. Not only was he recognized by the mountain biking community as a phenomenal athlete, but now he was recognized as one of the best riders in the world. Unwilling to rest for even an instant, Overend raced in the Iron Horse Classic, a race sponsored by his friend and former employer, Ed Zink. The race was held just hours before he caught his plane to the Hall of Fame induction ceremony in Somerville, New Jersey. In his acceptance speech, Overend describes the honor of joining the ranks of such notables as multiple Tour de France winner Greg LeMond, explaining, "I am thrilled to be included in the Bicycling Hall of Fame. I have followed the careers and been inspired by the accomplishments of this group and to be considered in the same league is an honor." [53]

Overend's Other Endeavors

Aside from being a husband, father, world mountain bike champ, and national triathlon winner, Overend also focuses on other activities. He currently works for Specialized in their bicycle research and development department, lending his sage advice to the design of future bikes and races. Overend enjoys his current work for Specialized, explaining "Whenever I go to a race I visit a few dealers, talking product, getting feedback, and take that info back to Specialized. I've been with Specialized a long time and I'm still as excited about being a part of them as I ever have been." [54] Overend is also part owner with Drew Boure of Boure Sportswear, a cycling clothing company based in Durango.

Overend's contribution to his sport extends to sharing his technical secrets in his book, *Mountain Bike Like a Champion,* coauthored with Ed Pavelka. In the book, Overend gives advice on training, technique, and racing. Overend also created an hour-long instructional video, *Performance Mountain Biking, The Basics and Beyond,* in which he gives tips and demonstrates techniques in clips featuring himself as well as some of the world's other top off-road cyclists. In a further effort to give back to the cycling community, Ned donated his winning XTERRA mountain bike and an assortment of gear to be auctioned by the International Mountain Bicycling Association (IMBA). Overend made the donation with the understanding that all proceeds from the auction would go to the Ned Overend Endowment, a fund to support trail building as well as lobbying efforts to maintain trail access for future generations of cyclists.

Ned Overend currently lives in Durango, Colorado. He still enters races when the time allows and the mood strikes him. He attributes his success and longevity to the balance he strives to achieve in life. He does not put his career before his family, and still participates in several sports, balancing business, workouts, family obligations, and rest with the precision of a master juggler. He also continues to talk about retiring someday, but adds that he will always ". . . stay involved with the industry, maybe do a little more snowboarding with my son, do some rock climbing or kayaking. . . . We live in a great place for all of those things." [55]

CHAPTER 6

Eric Jackson: A Strong Voice in the Kayaking Community

In the spring of 2001, Eric "EJ" Jackson pointed the nose of his kayak into the swirling vortex of whitewater as he rehearsed moves in his head. He had surfed his boat in this very spot a year earlier to win the Pre–World Championship in freestyle kayaking. But the water had not been so high then, and the stakes of that qualifying event were not so great. Jackson threw himself into the whirlpool over and over, executing spins and turns and cartwheels within its powerful clutches.

Jackson's score in the upcoming World Freestyle Kayaking contest would be judged on how well he performed each trick. He managed to spin one of his signature moves, a cartwheel with a 180-degree twist, before the current spit him out of the hole, capsizing his boat. With incredible precision, he positioned the paddle, and with a sharp twist of his hips, he was upright once more, pointing back into the maelstrom, determined to try again. A few powerful paddle strokes thrust the 5-foot, 6-inch, 160-pound muscular athlete back into the spot where he felt most comfortable, the center of a large, spinning wall of whitewater and foam. Jackson had his mind set on one thing: reclaiming his title as World Freestyle Champion.

Early Years

Eric Jackson was born on March 3, 1964, in Warren, Ohio, to parents James and Karen. He lived in Cincinnati until the age of three, when the family moved to Woolrich, Pennsylvania. His father, a retired military pilot, was an engineer at Piper Aircraft. Jackson's mother divided her time between taking care of the house and working at the Woolrich Woolen Mills as an accounts payable clerk.

Woolrich was a small, isolated town, so Jackson spent most of his time playing outdoors—riding motorcycles and building tree forts.

He had to hide these pursuits from his father, who sought to protect his son from harm. Since he was not allowed to play baseball or football due to the danger his father felt they presented, Jackson began swimming competitively at an early age, winning several butterfly stroke titles.

As a child, Jackson had lost half of his hearing when he became ill with scarlet fever. The family could not afford an expensive hearing aid, but Jackson was determined not to let hearing loss hold him back. "I always sat front and center [in class] and learned to lip read really well, which is responsible for 80% of what I take in during conversation. This really improved my social skills. I became very confident and was quite involved in everything I did, since I was always front and center." [56]

First Introduction to Paddling

Jackson's first paddling experience was in June 1970, on a canoe trip with his father and several work colleagues on Pennsylvania's Pine Creek. Six-year-old Jackson was immediately drawn to the one kayak

Eric Jackson raises his arms in victory after claiming the championship title at the 2001 World Freestyle Kayaking contest in Spain.

in the group. Although it would be nearly a decade before Jackson bought his own kayak, he knew from that moment on that he loved whitewater and wanted to spend as much time boating as possible.

Jackson loved paddling, and fortunately for him his father shared his love of canoeing. Drawn to the abundance of rivers in the northeastern United States, Jackson's parents relocated the family to New Hampshire. There, Jackson and his father bought two kayaks and began paddling every weekend. With this abundance of time on the river, the Jackson duo soon joined the Merrimac Valley Paddlers, a loose-knit group of novice and intermediate paddlers who met to discuss issues, practice moves, and run rivers. The two were not only accepted by the group, but soon became leaders. Jackson Sr., with his executive skills, became president, and Jackson Jr., an accomplished swimmer, taught new members how to roll capsized boats upright in swimming pools.

Building Confidence on Whitewater

During the first three years of kayaking with his father, Eric, nicknamed EJ, explored many northeastern rivers including the Sougheagan, the Kennebec, and the West River. As more experienced paddlers started inviting him to join them on more challenging rivers, Jackson began to realize not only his passion for the sport, but also his ability. He explains this realization: "Suddenly, I was discovering that I was one of the best boaters around, certainly the best in our club. I was a big fish in a little pond. . . . At this point, I was convinced that I was the best paddler out there and there was never any evidence otherwise." [57]

When he graduated from high school, Jackson, influenced by his father, entered the University of Maine's engineering program in 1982. There, he also joined the university's swimming team. The combination of study, team swimming, and paddling in his spare time, however, proved too challenging for Jackson. Then, in 1983, Jackson's mother died, serving as a catalyst for him to strike out on his own. He explains:

> My mother was the only person that kept the family together. My dad . . . didn't maintain any connection with me after my mother died. . . . He just related to me when I was there [at home] . . . and my mother was the only one who got me there. I started questioning all of the things I had committed to at that point in my life. . . . My dad wouldn't support me in school if I wasn't doing well, but he wasn't influencing me anymore. . . . I decided that I could break out of the mold, make my own path, as all winners in life did." [58]

Jackson decided to quit swimming and focus on kayaking for his extracurricular activity.

Jackson wanted not just to paddle, but to do so competitively. He had seen the uniformed members of the U.S. Slalom Kayak Team paddle past him on several occasions and now aspired to join this elite group. He entered his first contest, the Androscoggin Kayak Race, and won second place, only three seconds behind U.S. Team member Chris McCormick and one spot ahead of former member Chris Smith. The fact that he performed so well in his first race gave Jackson the confidence he needed to pursue his goal of becoming a competitive kayaker.

Jackson was drawn to slalom kayaking, which had been an established sport since 1949. This type of paddling involves a plotted course on a river, roughly 300–600 meters long. Paddlers weave in and out of twenty-five gates, both upstream and downstream. They receive a timed score with points deducted for each gate they touch. This form of paddling involves extensive training and top-notch boating skills. Slalom kayaking is an Olympic sport, and Jackson set his sights on one day competing in the Olympics.

An Opportunity to Train

Jackson contacted Bill Endicott, the U.S Slalom Team coach, and shared his ambition with him. Endicott, who already knew of EJ as the local boy who had given two of his team members a run for their money, invited Jackson to train with the team for a week to see if he had what it took to become a member. At the week's end, Jackson was invited to train in Maryland.

Deciding to take his training seriously, Jackson transferred to the University of Maryland in 1984. Jackson threw himself into the training routine, while continuing his engineering studies. James Jackson, however, did not support his son's activities and stopped providing money for them. Since his father no longer funded him, Jackson worked a series of odd jobs while studying and training. Coach Endicott recalls Jackson's determination and the lengths he was forced to go to in pursuit of his dreams, explaining, "He would run out of money in the spring and have to stop racing for a week or so to earn enough to keep going. But he never complained. [He was] . . . an incredible athlete who spent an amazing amount of time in the water. . . . Plus, he was endearing. He motivated you because he worked so hard." [59] Finally, however, tired of juggling school, work, and training, Jackson withdrew from the university in 1986 and began training full time, selling insurance to support himself.

Jackson (right) leads the pack downriver during a slalom kayaking race. Jackson's fearlessness and speed helped him earn a spot on the U.S. Slalom Team to compete in the 1992 Olympic Games.

Pressed to Settle Down

Jackson continued to work hard at training, but friends and family members pressed him to settle down into a full-time job and give up his dream. One person who encouraged Jackson to pursue his dream, however, was his girlfriend Kristine, whom he had met at a competition in 1987. The two dated for several months, and she continued to support him in his pursuit, even when Jackson failed to make the U.S. team for the fourth year.

This failure tested even Jackson's resolve. He was tired of putting so much effort into kayaking without achieving his goal and contemplated quitting. Kristine, however, knew that he was happiest when he was paddling, and encouraged him to quit his insurance job and work nights so that he could train harder. Jackson heeded her advice and took a job as a waiter. He paddled and trained by day, and worked most evenings. Kristine supported Eric emotionally, and in August of 1988 the two were married. Two years later, in 1990, the Jacksons had their first child, a girl named Emily.

Joining the U.S. Slalom Team

Finally, in 1989, five years of training paid off when Endicott invited Jackson to join the U.S. Slalom Team. Jackson soon proved just how good he was. His first year in competition he placed eleventh at the World Cup, an event that draws paddlers from around the world. While ten other slalom kayakers scored higher than Jackson, his was the highest score of any American in the competition. He placed tenth at the World Cup in 1990 and eleventh in 1991. Jackson's old dream finally came true when he was asked to compete in the Summer 1992 Olympics in Barcelona, Spain.

Jackson entered the Olympics with high hopes, but experienced two mishaps that cost him not just the gold, but any chance for a medal. First, while warming up for the race, he missed the start and had to paddle almost 500 meters just to reach the beginning of the course. Then, on his second attempt, he hit one of the slalom gates, which disqualified that run. Overall, he placed thirteenth among the Olympic competitors, although as had been true in the World Cup competition, he was first among the Americans. Jackson continued to race for the U.S. Slalom Team, although he had become interested in a new form of kayaking, freestyle, which was more reminiscent of his early paddling in the Northeast.

A New Type of Contest

Freestyle kayaking, or play boating, is a less rigid, training-intensive form of kayaking. Freestyle contests are often referred to as rodeos, because when the kayaker enters a whirlpool of water naturally formed by rocks or obstacles beneath the water's surface, the boat spins around wildly, like a bronco or a bull, in the vortex. The paddler in the hole can freely execute flips, spins, cartwheels, and a variety of other stunts.

Even as he had trained for the 1992 Olympics, Jackson had been intrigued by freestyle, partly because compared to slalom it was relatively unstructured. Sportswriter Mark Bechtel describes the lure of freestyle rodeo kayaking:

> Free of the rigid regulations of slalom, which is tightly controlled by the International Canoe Federation, freestyle shuns official rankings, and paddlers run their sport as a virtual democracy. If, for example, a paddler comes up with a new move, it is introduced and demonstrated to other freestylers, who vote on whether it should be accepted for use in competition.[60]

Contestants in freestyle competitions are given a certain amount of time, usually forty-five seconds, to perform as many different moves as they can. These moves are then judged and given a point rating according to their degree of difficulty and the boater's skill at executing each one. The paddler with the highest number of points totaled from all runs wins. Drawn to the less-structured format and the opportunity for sheer fun these competitions offered, Jackson began to enter freestyle in addition to slalom contests in 1993.

Experiencing Freestyle Success

Jackson quickly experienced success in freestyle, winning the White-water Rodeo World Championships in 1993. He had won several smaller freestyle contests already, but this win, Jackson notes, was important because "I showed up to my first freestyle world championships as somebody who didn't have a chance . . . and won. I was finally able to show off my play boating skills. It was an incredible boost to my self confidence since I had been trying to be number one in the world full time for 9 years and failed."[61]

The opportunity to show the paddling world what a versatile boater he was made this event one of Jackson's most memorable, but it was important to him for another reason as well. While freestyle still requires travel, the looser format of the freestyle event and lack of training involved enabled him to bring with him Kristine, Emily, and the latest addition to the Jackson family, a four-month-old baby boy, Dane. Dane had been born three months premature, and doctors said he had little likelihood of survival, but now he sat in his seat staring wide-eyed at the world of freestyle paddling.

Trying to Survive as a Professional Paddler

Bolstered by his victory in freestyle, Jackson once again set his sights on conquering slalom racing. He trained harder than ever, and won a number of contests, but injuries to the left side of his body sustained in the 1995 World Freestyle competitition forced him to take four months off from training to heal. This setback did not stop Jackson from setting his sights on qualifying for the 1996 Olympics, but part of him felt a pull toward the more carefree lifestyle of the freestyle whitewater paddler.

Jackson's dream of being the world's best slalom paddler was becoming a stressful full-time job and was physically draining with little payback. He no longer worked as a waiter, instead earning money by running his own paddling and climbing business called Adventure Schools. While working in outdoor education was more rewarding than his previous work, it was also a more challenging, time-consuming job.

Jackson decided to continue training, but times were tough and the money was scarce. To make ends meet, Jackson resorted to a variety of often-humorous fund-raising schemes. Bechtel describes some of Jackson's antics: "Making a living in slalom was next to impossible." He adds that Jackson started "going door to door . . . introducing himself as 'your local Olympic kayaker' and handing out newspaper clips and self-addressed stamped envelopes . . . (for) potential donors."[62] Another attempt at raising money for travel expenses to a competition found Jackson dressed in his Olympic uniform, pulling his kayak to street corners in Washington, D.C., and selling autographed copies of his picture to passersby. Though these events are funny anecdotes, this period of Jackson's life was a struggle to gain recognition and compensation for all of his hard work. While amusing, they were a serious attempt to keep his dream alive, since he had few sponsors and was not getting much in the way of prize money.

Reevaluating the Suburban Lifestyle

Despite his best efforts, Jackson did not make the cut for the 1996 Olympic team, and he was distraught over this failure. He was mad at himself for his poor performance, but most of his anger came from the feeling that he had been wrong to focus on slalom, rather than

Jackson practices a front loop spin. After failing to make the 1996 Olympic slalom team, he changed his competitive focus to the freestyle arena.

Jackson navigates a dangerous line around rapids and down a rocky waterfall. Jackson has become one of kayaking's most feared competitors, in both the slalom and freestyle disciplines.

listening to his inner voice, which had been telling him to pursue freestyle since his 1993 world victory. He felt as if this decision had stifled him and doomed him to a confined, suburban existence that involved a constant pursuit of money. With this thought in mind, Jackson decided to take several months off to paddle rivers for personal pleasure once more.

The time off allowed Jackson to finally let go of his anger at himself, and when he returned to competition, it was exclusively as a freestyle paddler. He took second place at the Ottawa World Freestyle competition in 1997. Still, despite this accomplishment, Jackson returned home somewhat depressed, wondering how he should focus his natural abundance of energy. Jackson again turned to his wife for support, and once again Kristine offered helpful words of advice, telling him they should abandon their attempt to fit into a suburban lifestyle. Jackson recalls of this advice,

> Kristine is the smartest of the two of us. She is also not afraid to just let go of what we have today and do something completely different. She suggested that we buy an RV and sell everything we own. . . . We decided that we were going mobile. I can't tell you how excited and relieved I felt. I was becoming a kayaker again. Just a kayaker, nothing else.[63]

Jackson sold Adventure Schools and bought a new thirty-one foot recreational vehicle (RV). The family of four packed the bare essentials and adopted a nomadic life in which Jackson could focus fully on finding the best water and training in beautiful surroundings around the world. Kristine, who had always been interested in teaching, began home schooling Dane and Emily. To earn money, Jackson taught paddling clinics. The new lifestyle solved the main problem with all of Jackson's training and competition in years past, which had been the amount of time he spent away from his family. Jackson describes the effect the change had on him, saying, "The family isn't like extra baggage. They blend in with the scene. We give the kayak scene hope. This can work." Kristine adds, "My life is great: the RV takes 10 minutes to clean, and I do a lot of things for myself, like read and run."[64]

Following the Seasons
Paddlers, by nature, follow a seasonal route, traveling to rivers that receive enough rainfall to provide whitewater and to regularly scheduled competitions. The Jacksons would travel from one competition to another during the summer, then go to Canada for August, where Jackson worked as a kayak instructor for Wilderness Tours on the Ottawa River. In the fall they would hit the East Coast for various whitewater festivals before traveling out of the country in winter to New Zealand, Australia, Costa Rica, and Africa. In the spring, the Jackson family would return to the East Coast for a month-long layover in North Carolina, where Jackson designed boats for Wave Sport Kayaks. The money from his various jobs, winnings from competitions, and sponsorship from a variety of companies was enough to support the family's nomadic lifestyle,

traveling from one beautiful spot to another doing the things Eric loved the most: socializing with family and friends, teaching, and winning contests.

Although Jackson still entered slalom races, he focused most of his attention on freestyle competitions. No longer aspiring to compete in the Olympics, Jackson gave up the strict training regimen he had followed for over ten years, and simply focused on paddling rivers, averaging thirty new rivers each year. Still, Jackson won twenty-seven contests, a mix of slalom and freestyle events, in 1998. He continued to design and test boats for Wave Sport, and took over as director of their design department. The company showed their appreciation with a steady paycheck, entry fees to competitions, and a brand new RV with a huge picture of Jackson on the side of it.

Returning to Civilization a Winner

Finally all of Jackson's efforts bore fruit in the World Freestyle Competition for 2001 in Spain. The Jackson family arrived weeks before the contest to recover from jet lag and allow Eric time to practice on

Jackson stands in front of his RV with his son, Dane, and daughter, Emily. The Jackson family lived on the road for many years while Eric competed, trained, and taught kayaking clinics.

the large hole that would serve as the course. In the competition, Jackson reclaimed the title of World Freestyle Champion.

When the family returned to the United States that year, they decided to put their wayward lifestyle on hold and settled about sixty miles southeast of Nashville in Rock Island, Tennessee. Their new house was built on twenty acres of land near some of Jackson's favorite freestyle boating rapids on both the Caney Fork and Ocoee Rivers. He could now train year-round near his own hometown without having to travel so much. The family still owns and uses the RV, attending contests all over North America and feeling at home wherever they go.

Eric Jackson wears many hats, all of them revolving in some way around the whitewater community. He founded the World Kayak Federation to raise support and donations for freestyle kayak competitions. He has written several instructional kayaking books, and produced a *Strokes and Concepts* video as a resource to paddlers as well. Still acting director of kayak design at Wave Sport, he has designed many of the top freestyle kayaks on the market, swearing that the company makes the best boats for rodeo kayaking. He also set his sights on the 2003 World Championships in Austria. Jackson considers himself lucky to be able to kayak full time, focus on his family, and give back to the paddling community as much as possible. Jackson claims his philosophy is "all about quality of life, having the most fun. If you can do that in such a way that it adds to the quality of other people's lives, then you're a real winner." [65]

NOTES

Chapter 1: Bob Burnquist: Master of the Switch Stance

1. Quoted in Emerson Brown, "The Boy from Brazil," *Switch Magazine*. www.switchmagazine.com.
2. Quoted in "Bob Burnquist Interview Part II," *Skateboarding*. www.skateboarding.com.
3. Quoted in Alec Wilkinson, "Bob Burnquist," *Rolling Stone*, June 10, 1999, p. 105.
4. Quoted in Matt Higgins, "Ramped Up," *Sports Illustrated for Kids*, August 2002, p. 27.
5. Quoted in "Bob Burnquist Interview Part II."
6. Quoted in Kevin Wilkins, "Any 1 Thing," *Transworld Skateboarding*, September 2001, p. 92.
7. Quoted in "An Interview with Bob Burnquist," Tripod.com. http://cgi.tripod.com.
8. Quoted in Joel Patterson, "Bob Burnquist," *Transworld Skateboarding*, August/September 2000, p. 37.
9. Quoted in Kevin Wilkins, "Other Than," *Transworld Skateboarding*, July 2002, p. 27.
10. Quoted in Brown, "The Boy from Brazil."
11. Quoted in "Bob Burnquist Signs Deal with Activision," Skateboarding Directory. http://skateboardingdirectory.com.
12. Quoted in Patterson, "Bob Burnquist."
13. Quoted in Matt Higgins, "Q&A Skateboard Superstar Bob Burnquist," *Sports Illustrated for Kids*, July 11, 2002. www.sikids.com.

Chapter 2: Terje Haakonsen: King of the Half Pipe

14. Quoted in Franz Lidz, "Lord of the Board," *Sports Illustrated*, December 22, 1997, p. 114–18.
15. Quoted in Lidz, "Lord of the Board."
16. Quoted in Karl Taro Greenfield, "Adjustment in Midflight," *Outside Online*, February 1999. web.outsideonline.com.
17. Quoted in Current Biography Electronic, "Terje Haakonsen," H.W. Wilson, 1998. www.hwwilson.com.

18. Dave Sypniewski, "The Legendary Mount Baker Banked Slalom," *Transworld Snowboarding,* December 27, 2000.

19. Quoted in Lidz, "Lord of the Board."

20. Quoted in Lidz, "Lord of the Board."

21. Quoted in Lidz, "Lord of the Board."

22. Quoted in Current Biography Electronic,"Terje Haakonsen."

23. Quoted in Karl Taro Greenfield, "Adjustment in Midflight," Outside Online, February 1999. web.outsideonline.com.

24. Quoted in Rene and Niklas Rodun, "Kicking Ass Viking Style," *Transworld Snowboarding,* February 9, 2000. www.transworld snowboarding.com.

25. Quoted in Rene and Niklas Rodun, "Kicking Ass Viking Style."

26. Quoted in Greenfield, "Adjustment in Midflight."

Chapter 3: Kelly Slater: World Champion Surfer

27. Quoted in Austin Murphy, "Back on Board," *Sports Illustrated,* February 18, 2002.

28. Quoted in Tad Friend, "The Workaday Adventures of a Barefoot Boy Millionaire and His Girl Next Door," *Outside Online,* May, 1999. http://web.outsideonline.com.

29. Quoted in Friend, "The Workaday Adventures."

30. Quoted in Friend, "The Workaday Adventures."

31. Quoted in Friend, "The Workaday Adventures."

32. Quoted in Brad Goldfarb, "Chairman of the Board," *Interview Magazine,* March 1996, p. 103.

33. Quoted in *Transworld Surf,* "Kelly Slater Outside the Boundaries," June 4, 2001.

34. Quoted in Todd Kline, "Kelly Slater," *Transworld Surf,* November 2002.

35. Quoted in Goldfarb, "Chairman of the Board."

Chapter 4: Lynn Hill: A Free Climbing Revolutionary

36. Quoted in "El Capitan's Nose Climbed Free," *American Alpine Journal,* 1994, Lynn Hill. www.stanford.edu.

37. Quoted in *Outside Online,* "Lynn Hill: Lessons of Stone," July 1, 1996. http://web.outsideonline.com.

38. Lynn Hill with Greg Child, *Climbing Free: My Life in the Vertical World*. New York: W.W. Norton, 2001, p. 103.

39. Hill, *Climbing Free,* p. 143.

40. Lynn Hill, "Journeys on the Rock," *Voices from the Summit: The World's Greatest Mountaineers on the Future of Climbing,* ed. Bernadette McDonald. Washington, DC: Adventure Press National Geographic, 2000, p. 113.

41. Hill, *Climbing Free,* p. 241.

42. Hill, *Climbing Free,* p. 246.

43. Hill, *Climbing Free,* p. 246.

44. Quoted in Mountainzone.com, "Lynn Hill: Climbing Through the Glass Ceiling," 1999. http://classic.mountainzone.com.

45. Hill, "Journeys on the Rock," p. 113.

46. Hill, "Journeys on the Rock," p. 113.

Chapter 5: Ned Overend: The Father of Mountain Bike Racing

47. Ned Overend, interview with author via e-mail, March 15, 2003.

48. Quoted in Stephen Malley, "Cycling: Right Away You Notice His Legs," *Sports Illustrated,* November 4, 1991.

49. Quoted in Malley, "Cycling."

50. Quoted in *MTBReview,* "Ned Overend Q&A." www.mtbreview.com.

51. Quoted in Zapata Espinoza, "O Captain, My Captain," *Mountain Bike,* December 1996.

52. Quoted in Zapata Espinoza, "Third Time's the Charm: Ned and X-Terra," *Mountain Bike,* March 1999.

53. Quoted in *Mountain Bike,* "Honoring the Lung," June 4, 2001.

54. Quoted in Dean Howard Fotografix, "Ned Overend Interview." www.deanhoward.com.

55. Quoted in "Ned Overend Interview."

Chapter 6: Eric Jackson: A Strong Voice in the Kayaking Community

56. Eric Jackson, e-mail interview with author, February 22, 2003.

57. Eric Jackson, "E.J.: My Kayaking Career," Eric Jackson Official Website, www.jacksonkayak.com.

58. Eric Jackson, e-mail interview with author, February 22, 2003.

59. Quoted in Beth Geiger. "They Call Him EJ," Paddling.com. http://paddling.about.com.

60. Quoted in Mark Bechtel, "Eric Jackson," *Sports Illustrated,* May 28, 2001, p. A4.

61. Jackson, "E.J.: My Kayaking Career."

62. Quoted in Bechtel, "Eric Jackson."

63. Jackson, "E.J.: My Kayaking Career."

64. Quoted in Geiger, "They Call Him EJ."

65. Quoted in Geiger, "They Call Him EJ."

FOR FURTHER READING

Books

Scott Bass, *Surf! Your Guide to Longboarding, Shortboarding, Tubing, Aerials, Hanging Ten, and More.* Washington, DC: National Geographic Society, 2003. This small book explains the basics of surfing with a brief synopsis of surf culture. It also profiles Kelly Slater in a brief section on professional surfing and contests.

Nicky Crowther, *The Ultimate Mountain Bike Book: The Definitive Guide to Bikes, Components, Techniques, Thrills, and Trails.* Willowdale, Ontario: Firefly Books, 2002. This book gives a brief history of the evolution of mountain biking. It mentions Ned Overend's entry into the hall of fame and gives a good overview of the sport.

Susanna Howe, *Sick: A Cultural History of Snowboarding.* New York: St. Martin's Griffin, 1998. This book gives a detailed history of snowboarding. It features descriptions of the Mount Baker Banked Slalom, Olympic boycotts and controversy, with pictures and comments on Terje Haakonsen.

Eric Jackson, *Whitewater Paddling Strokes and Concepts.* Mechanicsburg, PA: Stackpole Books, 1999. In this book, top paddler Eric Jackson gives advice on kayaking for beginners and intermediates.

Drew Kampion, *Stoked: A History of Surf Culture.* Los Angeles: General Publishing Group, 1997. This book gives a detailed history of surfing and surf culture. It contains several pages on Kelly Slater and his impact on professional surfing.

Joe Layden, *Burton Snowboarders' Pro Riders: No Limits.* New York: Scholastic, 2001. This book gives a brief history of snowboarding and details several Pro Burton Snowboarders including Terje Haakonsen.

Joy Masoff, *Snowboard! Your Guide to Freeriding Pipe and Park, Jibbing, Backcountry, Alpine, Boardercross, and More.* Washington, DC: National Geographic Society, 2002. This book explains the basics of snowboarding with a brief synopsis of snowboard culture, the Extreme Games, and the Olympics.

Marilyn Olsen, *Women Who Risk: Profiles of Women in Extreme Sports.* New York: Hatherleigh, 2003. This book contains a fifteen-page profile of Lynn Hill and her climbing history.

Ned Overend with Ed Pavelka, *Mountain Bike Like a Champion.* Emmaus, PA: Rodale, 1999. This book contains techniques and tips from top cyclist Ned Overend. It is broken into three sections: core concepts, advanced mountain biking, and competititon.

Pete Takeda, *Climb! Your Guide to Bouldering, Sport Climbing, Trad Climbing, Ice Climbing, Alpinism, and More.* Washington, DC: National Geographic Society, 2002. This book explains the basics of rock climbing with focus on both sport climbing and big wall climbing. It contains a brief profile and pictures of Lynn Hill.

Videos

ESPN's Ultimate X, Dir. Bruce Hendricks. 2002. 39 mins.

Free Climbing the Nose, Dir. Lynn Hill. 1994. 25 mins.

Ned Overend, Performance Mountain Biking, Dir. John C. Davis. 1996. 58 mins.

Subjekt Haakonsen—Life and Times of a Sprocking Cat, Dir. Dave Seaone. 1996. 30 mins.

The Haakonsen Faktor, Dir. Dave Seaone. 1999. 24 mins.

Websites

Eric Jackson's Official Website (www.jacksonkayak.com). This is kayaker Eric Jackson's homepage. It includes his paddling history and other stories about his family, friends, and adventures. This site also has a section on paddling techniques and an online store where you can purchase Jackson's book.

Ned Overend's Home Page (www.boure.com/ned.html). This website contains Ned's bio, article links, career results, and race journal. It also contains travel and cycling links to Durango, Colorado, and Ned's company, Boure Cycling.

Quiksilver Home Page (www.quiksilver.com). This site has details on surfing, skateboarding, and snowboarding. Kelly Slater is a member of the Quicksilver team, so it has links to information on him as well.

WORKS CONSULTED

Books

Lynn Hill, "Journeys on the Rock," *Voices from the Summit: The World's Greatest Mountaineers on the Future of Climbing*. Ed. Bernadette McDonald. Washington, DC: Adventure Press National Geographic, 2000. This series of essays from famous rock climbers and mountaineers gives personal accounts of historic climbs and questions the future of rock climbing as a sport.

Lynn Hill with Greg Child, *Climbing Free: My Life in the Vertical World*. New York: W.W. Norton, 2001. Personal memoir and autobiography of Lynn Hill's rock climbing history. This book includes her account of the historic Nose climb.

Periodicals

Mark Bechtel, "Eric Jackson," *Sports Illustrated*, May 28, 2001.

Zapata Espinoza, "O Captain, My Captain," *Mountain Bike*, December 1996.

———, "Third Time's the Charm: Ned and XTERRA." *Mountain Bike*, March 1999.

Brad Goldfarb, "Chairman of the Board," *Interview Magazine*, May 1996.

Matt Higgins, "Ramped Up," *Sports Illustrated for Kids*, August 2002.

Todd Kline, "Kelly Slater," *Transworld Surf*, November 2002.

Franz Lidz, "Lord of the Board," *Sports Illustrated*, December 22, 1997.

Stephen Malley, "Cycling: Right Away You Notice His Legs." *Sports Illustrated*, November 4, 1991.

Ken McAlpine, "King of the Hill," *Sports Illustrated for Kids*, January 1998.

Austin Murphy, "Back on Board," *Sports Illustrated*, February 18, 2002.

Joel Patterson, "Bob Burnquist," *Transworld Skateboarding*, August/ September 2000.

Dave Sypniewski, "The Legendary Mount Baker Banked Slalom," *Transworld Snowboarding*, December 27, 2000.

Kevin Wilkins, "Any 1 Thing," *Transworld Skateboarding*, September 2001.

———, "Other Than," *Transworld Skateboarding*, July 2002.

Alec Wilkinson, "Bob Burnquist," *Rolling Stone*, June 10, 1999.

Internet Sources

Emerson Brown, "The Boy from Brazil," Switch Magazine. www.switch magazine.com.

Current Biography Electronic, "Terje Haakonsen," H.W. Wilson, 1998. www.hwwilson.com.

Dean Howard Fotografix, "Ned Overend Interview," www.dean howard.com.

Tad Friend, "The Workaday Adventures of a Barefoot Boy Millionaire and His Girl Next Door," Outside Online, May 1999. http://web. outsideonline.com.

Beth Geiger, "They Call Him EJ," Paddling.com. http://paddling. about.com.

Karl Taro Greenfield, "Adjustment in Midflight," Outside Online, February 1999. http://web.outsideonline.com.

Matt Higgins, "Q&A Skateboard Superstar Bob Burnquist," Sports Illustrated for Kids, July 11, 2002. www.sikids.com.

Lynn Hill, "El Capitan's Nose Climbed Free," American Alpine Journal, 1994. www.stanford.edu.

Eric Jackson, "E.J.: My Kayaking Career," Eric Jackson Official Website. www.jacksonkayak.com.

Mountainzone.com, "Lynn Hill: Climbing Through the Glass Ceiling," 1999. http://classic.mountainzone.com.

MTB Journal, "Ned Enters Bicycling Hall of Fame," June 4, 2001. http://www.mtbjournal.com.

MTBReview, "Ned Overend Q&A," 2001. www.mtbreview.com.

Outside Online, "Lynn Hill: Lessons of Stone," July 1, 1999. http://web. outsideonline.com.

Rene and Niklas Rodun, "Kicking Ass Viking Style," Transworld Snowboarding, February 9, 2000. http://www.transworldsnowboarding.com.

Skateboard Directory, "Bob Burnquist Signs Deal with Activision, August 8, 2002. http://skateboarddirectory.com

Skateboarding Magazine, "Bob Burnquist Interview Part II." www.skate boarding.com.

Transworld Surf, "Kelly Slater Outside the Boundaries," June 4, 2001. http://expn.go.com.

Tripod.com, "An Interview with Bob Burnquist," March 1999. http://members.tripod.com.

INDEX

action sports, 11
Activision, 22
Adventure Schools, 92
aid climbing, 66
Anderson, Pamela, 57
Anti-Hero (skateboard
  company), 18, 20–21
Arctic Challenge
  (snowboarding), 49–50
Association of Surfing
  Professionals (ASP), 57
athletes, characteristics of great,
  9–11

Basham, Doug, 75–76
Baywatch (TV series), 57
Bechtel, Mark, 91, 93
bike racing. *See* mountain bike
  racing; road bike racing
Bludworth, Chuck, 64–65
Boure, Drew, 85
Buffet Froid route (rock
  climbing), 69
Burnquist, Bob (Robert Dean
  Silva)
  as actor, 22
  awards and honors, 19, 22
  competitions, 17–18, 21–22
  education, 13–14, 18
  fame, 22–23
  family, 13, 19–20
  financial endeavors, 20, 24
  health, 13, 15
  on importance of
    skateboarding, 24
  innovations by, 11, 16, 21–22
  interests of, 23
  as role model, 20, 23–24
  skateboarding style of, 16

sponsors of, 16, 18, 20–21, 22
turned professional, 15–16
video games and, 22–23
youth, 13–15
Burnquist, Dean (father), 13, 19,
  20
Burnquist, Dora (mother), 13,
  19, 20
Burnquist, Lotus O'Brien Silva
  (daughter), 19–20
Burnquist, Milena (sister), 13,
  20
Burnquist, Rebecca (sister), 13
Burnquist Organics, 20, 24
Burton, Jake, 28
Burton Snowboards, 32, 50

Cabalerial (snowboarding), 28
catching big air (snowboarding),
  26
Changing Corners route (rock
  climbing), 70–71, 72
competitions
  multisport, 76, 82–84
  see also specific sports
Coors Classic (road bike race),
  77
Curren, Tom, 61

Deadly Nedly, 80

El Capitan (Yosemite National
  Park), 63, 66–67, 70–74
Endicott, Bill, 89, 91
Endless Summer, The (film), 57
EXTREME (film), 50, 52

father of mountain bike racing.
  See Overend, Ned

PICTURE CREDITS

ABOUT THE AUTHOR

Ron Horton is an English teacher and freelance writer who lives in Portland, Oregon. Ron grew up exploring the Blue Ridge Mountains of Virginia and North Carolina. In his spare time, he enjoys rock climbing, snowboarding, and fly-fishing with his black Labrador, Cody.